# "You haven't given me your answer, Liane."

Liane stood there wondering why she hesitated like this. She'd been in love with Richard for almost as long as she'd worked for him. She had longed for this moment. So, why was she hesitating?

Suddenly, leaping into her consciousness, was that scene in the glade in South Africa—Flint's passionate kisses, his strong arms embracing her, his tenderness and his words, "Darling Liane, will you...."

She had stopped him, but those words of his had followed his declaration that he wanted her for his wife. Liane recalled how she had wished it was Richard.

Well, she had only to say the word now. Instead, she was remembering how it was when she'd been alone with Flint. What was she trying to tell herself?

# Harbour of Love

by

## ANNE HAMPSON

*Harlequin Books*

TORONTO • LONDON • NEW YORK • AMSTERDAM
SYDNEY • HAMBURG • PARIS

Original hardcover edition published in 1977
by Mills & Boon Limited

ISBN 0-373-02230-1

Harlequin edition published January 1979

# CHAPTER ONE

SEVERAL dark blue butterflies caught Liane's attention and her pensive eyes followed them until they disappeared into the dazzling mosaic of flowers that occupied a far corner of the garden.

She was standing on the back stoep and after a few moments of brooding loneliness she turned her eyes towards the house visible through the trees, a long white homestead built on the lines of the Dutch-style houses which had originated in the Cape vineyards. At the front and sides were shady stoeps each with a gabled palisade along which masses of sub-tropical flowers spread a miracle of colour contrasts and heady perfumes. Smooth verdant lawns on the north, east and south were enhanced by spreading oak and mahogany trees spaced at irregular intervals, their sun-tinted foliage dancing in the breeze. On a spacious flagged area surrounding the man-made waterfall and pool were large ornamental pots containing palms of many varieties, some brought from places like Barbados and the Orient. A lovely fragrant litsea grew in another large urn, and next to it was a lotus-flowered magnolia.

Liane's large, widely-spaced eyes took on a brooding expression as unhappy thoughts intruded, remind-

ing her of a handsome face and a charming smile ...
and her own unrequited love.

'Liane! Come and get it!' The carefree, laughing
voice belonged to Liane's cousin Kirsty who, having
met and fallen in love with a South African while
holidaying in Durban, had married him six months
ago and was now the proud mistress of Gimbulu Farm,
his small but thriving estate set in the valley of a
tributary of the Limpopo River.

'Thanks, Kirsty.' Liane managed a cheerful smile as
she took possession of a chair at the daintily-laid table
where a salad and cold meat had been prepared by
Sylvester, the dusky-faced houseboy who, along with
Lulu, the girl who came in three times a week to do
the washing and cooking, relieved Kirsty of all domestic chores. 'Where's Mark?'

'Still in the bathroom, getting rid of all that sweat
and dust he collected while he was out there in the
mealie field.' Picking up the plate of bread and butter,
she silently invited Liane to help herself. 'He says we
must begin without him.'

Liane took the bread, put it on her side-plate before
picking up her knife and fork.

'That house over there—Kimara Lodge—looks
most attractive. It's owned by a bachelor living alone,
you said?' Liane spoke merely to make conversation,
keeping her mind on the present and hoping the past
and the future would not intrude.

'Yes, Flint Dawson, our neighbour. He owns vast
timber forests and citrus fruit plantations.' A sudden
twinkle of fun entered her big hazel eyes as she added,
'His name suits him, especially when he's in one of his
more inflexible moods. It suits his eyes, too. They're

hard, and dark grey in colour, and when you look deeply into them you feel that their owner is just about as tough as they come!'

'He sounds rather unattractive,' commented Liane without much interest as she concentrated on cutting a piece of meat ready to put into her mouth. 'Do you see much of him?'

'He rides over quite regularly, as a matter of fact. I wouldn't agree that he's unattractive,' Kirsty went on. 'The women who frequent the Sunset Club in Ravensville all seem to be crazy about him—very eligible, he is, in a place where single males are scarce.'

'He has no special girl-friend?'

'Alma Moulton, a pale-skinned beauty with a willowy figure and a deep husky voice that men seem to find attractive. To me, she sounds like a horse with adenoids——' Kirsty broke off as Liane burst out laughing. 'There are some who declare quite firmly that she'll get him, and others who say she's not his type at all. Well, it's all conjecture at the moment, but I'll say this : whoever does land our handsome neighbour for a husband will have to resign herself to being kept right under his thumb. He's ever so bossy.'

'He's becoming even more unattractive.'

'You'll be judging for yourself tomorrow evening. He's invited us over for a sundowner.'

'He has?' with a trace of interest now. 'You didn't mention this before?'

'I was coming round to it. He called this afternoon while you were out exploring the river bank. He expressed regret that he hadn't met you and immediately invited us over to Kimara Lodge—tomorrow evening, as I said. Okay with you?'

'Yes, of course. What does one have to wear?'

'Nothing formal; it's not like one of his fabulous dinner parties where all the females try to outshine one another with their long evening gowns. For a sundowner you don't bother much. Wear one of those pretty summer dresses you've brought with you.' A softer note had unconsciously entered Kirsty's voice. Aware of Liane's unhappiness, Kirsty had been making a deliberate effort to divert her mind from Richard. Flint's invitation had been gladly accepted by Kirsty, whose instant reaction was that this small social event would provide a pleasant and diverting interlude for her cousin. Liane, glancing at her across the table, and having noticed the softer tone, knew that beneath the gay exterior there was deep compassion in her cousin's make-up.

Pity . . .? Liane did not want it. Moreover, she freely owned that she did not deserve it. Falling in love with her boss had been foolish, her own fault entirely, since Richard Wilding had never once—to Liane's knowledge—noticed her as a woman. By his own telling, which she had once overheard, Liane was 'the most efficient and accommodating woman I have ever met'. And he had gone on to say that he had been exceedingly fortunate when he engaged her as his secretary.

For six years she had been his secretary; they were years of devotion, of service, of sacrifice, even, since she never hesitated to cancel an engagement if Richard should require her on some project of his own as, for example, on that occasion when, her summer holiday booked, she had instantly cancelled it when he had asked her to accompany him to a conference which he

8

was attending in the north of England. Liane now knew that everything she did was taken for granted by her boss, but she knew also that there was a most attractive side to his nature and had she been able to penetrate the hard exterior of the businessman she would have discovered all she desired in a husband. It had taken the beautiful and sophisticated Marlene Saville to pierce the armour of the man who was the epitome of the prosperous business magnate and find the treasure within. Whether or not Marlene would continue to appreciate that treasure was a debatable point as far as Liane was concerned. Outwardly Marlene was wonderful with Richard who, having reached the age of forty without once having been involved in a serious love affair, became a totally different man under the warmth of Marlene's attention. But as a friend of Liane's once said, it takes a woman to read another woman, and Liane was deeply troubled that the man she loved would one day meet with disillusionment.

'You're dreaming, pet.' The softly-spoken words of her cousin brought Liane's mind back to the present and she smiled faintly and reached for another piece of bread and butter. 'It's done, Liane,' added Kirsty, 'and so it's best if you can accept it. Otherwise, you're going to have to change your job.'

'I'm not right down in the depths of despair,' Liane assured her. 'It's just that I feel, quite often, that I missed my opportunity. I had Richard to myself for six years, remember——' She broke off, and gave a small regretful sigh. 'I wasn't very clever, Kirsty. Six years!—and I hadn't the nous to learn how to make him notice me as a woman, and not a super-efficient robot that sprang into action immediately he pressed a button. Apart from taking a great deal of trouble to acquire a dress sense, and thereafter wearing only what—in my opinion—flattered me, I did precious little to attract his attention in the way I wanted to attract it.' Again she sighed, thinking of the way Marlene had, in a matter of weeks, achieved what Liane herself had been trying to achieve since she was nineteen. And now, at twenty-five, she was fully resigned to spinsterhood, since she could not, by any stretch of imagination, see any other man taking Richard's place in her heart.

'It's because you're no vamp, that's what it is,' Kirsty was saying loyally. 'But, Liane,' she went on, 'if it were meant to be that you and Richard would get together then he'd have fallen in love without any encouragement from you. Love would have come to him naturally, as it did to Mark and me. And it would have come quickly.'

Liane nodded her agreement and no more was said about Richard Wilding. However, Liane was still of the opinion that she had missed her chance and, the way she felt at this moment, she was sure she would never fully recover from the shock she had received on that blackest day of her life when, after casually calling her into his office, Richard had instructed her to insert the announcement of his engagement in the newspaper. Liane had just stared, while her notebook fluttered from her trembling hand to the floor, and in her heart something died.

'We shall be away for the first two weeks in September,' he had gone on in that cool impersonal voice she knew so well. 'But you'll manage in your usual efficient way to deal with any emergencies. Marlene wants me to meet her mother, who lives in Bermuda. Perhaps you'll contact a travel agent and sort out the flights and hotels and anything else you might think of.' He had smiled then, that smile that had always sent a ripple of pleasure through her whole body. 'I'm very fortunate, Liane, in having someone like you to take the responsibility for all these things—— Oh, by the way, will you see to the servicing of my car? Phone Wrights, but don't let them keep it for more than a day.' He had smiled again, but on this never-to-be-forgotten day his smiles brought a pain so fierce that she had gone home to her tiny flat in Kingston and wept with all the abandonment of utter despair. And then she had spent the rest of the evening trying to make up her mind whether or not to leave the firm and seek a post elsewhere, a long way away so that there would be no possibility of her ever coming across Richard again ... or his wife. But in the end his dependence upon her proved to be the deciding factor and she expelled from her mind the idea of handing in her notice. Yet she found herself wishing something would happen, something sufficiently diverting to carry her through this dark period of her life.

And as if in answer to a prayer a letter had arrived, less than a week later, containing an invitation from her cousin for her to spend a holiday with Kirsty and her husband at their farm in South Africa.

'Come just when you like (I know that boss of yours will be sure to mess up your normal vacation) and stay for as long as you possibly can. You'll adore our home, and both Mark and I shall love having you.'

Liane had immediately begun to reckon up the holi-

11

days she had owing to her, studying herself for the very first time since she had become secretary to Richard. There was a three-week break owing to her from last year; she added this on to the week she should have had at Easter and the two weeks she was intending to take in October, the month which, Richard said, would suit his needs better than the first two weeks in July, the period originally chosen by Liane because a friend had asked her to go on a cruise with her at that time.

Richard had just stared at Liane as if she were mad when, having calmly told him of her acceptance of her cousin's invitation, she had then said she would be away for six weeks.

'Six weeks!' he had ejaculated, taking a real interest in her for the first time. 'How in heaven's name am I going to manage?' His brown eyes became soft for once, and almost pleading.

Pale but composed, she had stood firm. If her plan did not meet with his approval she would hand in her notice. This she told him, in a quiet but determined tone of voice, and the words were hardly out of her mouth when he capitulated, agreeing that she needed a long holiday and she must certainly have it. He had been selfish and unthinking, and his sincere apology took the form of his including a most generous bonus in the pay packet she received the following week, which was the end of the month and just a few days before she was to fly out to South Africa.

'Have a good time, Liane,' he had smiled, sparing her a few moments when she entered his office to say goodbye. And then, with that total honesty which was as much a part of him as his business acumen, he admitted he would be lost without her, and he had added finally,

'I must confess, Liane, that I shall be happy indeed on the day you return to the office.'

'Liane, you look absolutely ravishing!' Kirsty, having knocked, and entered the charming pink and white bedroom occupied by her cousin, stood well back and surveyed her appraisingly. 'That shade of blue goes delectably with your eyes! And that dainty brocade trimming—— Yes, you were right when you said you'd learned to wear only what flattered you!'

Kirsty's enthusiastic comments naturally brought a flush to Liane's cheeks, but at the same time they encouraged another glance into the mirror, and Liane's eyes went automatically to it. The dress, of crisp linen with a brocade trimming of a paler shade of blue, had a high neckline with small points all around it forming a narrow collar. Nipped in at the waist, and with a skirt which flared out while not being in any way too full, it enhanced the graceful lines of her figure just as its colour enhanced the alabaster of her skin and accentuated the liquid radiance of her eyes.

'Thank you, Kirsty,' she said quietly at last, turning to cast her own appreciative glance over the charming picture which her cousin made. She wore a flowered tunic over white cotton slacks; her light brown hair, brushed back from her heart-shaped face, was secured by a bow of white ribbon. The small white and rose earrings and matching necklace were presents which Liane had brought out from England when she came to Gimbulu Farm three days previously. 'You too look exceedingly attractive.'

Kirsty laughed and her brown eyes shone. Her sheer undiluted happiness was wonderful to see, thought Liane ... but it brought back her own situation, and her hopeless love for Richard.

'Are you ready, darling?' Kirsty called to her husband who was in the bedroom putting on a newly-laundered pair of lightweight slacks and an open-necked shirt.

'I shall be in just one minute from now,' he returned.

He appeared presently, a man of medium height with homely bronzed features and wide powerful shoulders. He had a ready, winning smile which, appearing frequently, gave evidence of the good humour and even temper so characteristic of him. Having taken to him on sight, Liane found him very pleasant company, always cheerful, and possessing an uncomplicated disposition which was so vastly different from that of Richard, whose hours of work were spent in a London office, while Mark's were spent in the peace and tranquillity of the wide open spaces.

'Shall we go across the fields or shall we go by car?' he inquired of his wife. Kirsty looked at Liane.

'I don't mind which way we go,' said Liane obligingly. 'Is it simpler to walk?'

'I think so,' from Kirsty. 'It'll take only about five or six minutes if we take the field path. It's longer by road, of course.'

'It might be raining when we're coming home,' warned Mark. 'You know how swiftly a storm gathers here.'

'I'm willing to risk it,' Kirsty told him. 'What about you, Liane, and that treasure of a dress?'

14

'It won't melt if it gets wet,' she laughed, and so it was decided that they walk across the fields.

Twilight was beginning to steal the blue from the sky as they entered the grounds of Flint Dawson's house by a low gate set in a pink and white oleander hedge. They stepped immediately on to a flagged path bordered by an interfusion of glorious colour provided by poppies, antirrhinums and nasturtiums, all in abandoned disarray, as if a gardener had placed the seeds in a bag, shaken it up, then carelessly scattered its contents along both sides of the path. This path led to that part of the homestead not visible from Gimbulu Farm. Liane, who had always had a delicate sense of what was beautiful, stood for a moment in silent appreciation, her eyes wandering from the gracefully-curving gables above the green-shuttered windows, to the stoep with its decorative floor tiles and vine-trellised roof, from where glowed a soft amber radiance, although the source of this was subtly hidden from view.

She turned her head to say something to her companions, but at that moment the owner of the house appeared from somewhere in the garden, a tall and sinewed Afrikaner dressed in a casual white jacket and slacks, his long easy strides covering the intervening distance with the grace and silence of a jungle cat.

'So you're right on time.' He stood head and shoulders above Liane, his eyes moving from her upturned face towards Kirsty, as he waited for the introduction. 'Happy to meet you, Miss Goulden.' His grip hurt and automatically she glanced down at his fingers; they were long and lean and coffee brown, like his face, proclaiming him to be a man of the great outdoors.

15

She returned his greeting, remembering her impression that she would find him somewhat unattractive—in his manner, that was, not his physical appearance. His voice had been polite but cool, his dark grey eyes, unmoving beneath their hooded lids, were coldly impersonal, as was his expression and the shaft of a smile he had given her.

The drinks were served by Kamau, Flint Dawson's houseboy, who was in reality a gaunt, middle-aged man with white hair and a stoical expression on his thin, heavily-lined face. He had been with Flint's parents, having come to them when he was only twelve years of age.

Conversation was general and light, with Kirsty doing rather more than her share of talking, her voice becoming noticeably animated whenever she mentioned her husband. This, Liane was quick to notice, several times brought a sardonic smile to Flint's face and she fell to wondering if he were cynical about love and marriage. He was thirty-four, Kirsty had said, so obviously he had not been in any hurry to give up his freedom.

'Kirsty tells me you're here for six weeks only,' Flint said at length in the polite manner of the host, and Liane, whose concentration had been on the change of scene as the veil of dusk enfolded the distant line of kopjes, turned her head towards him and in response to his politeness gave him a slow and charming smile as she said yes, this was correct. 'It isn't long enough,' Flint told her, and she nodded her head in agreement.

'I'm so bewitched with this place already,' she confessed. 'It's so primitive and restful, and Gimbulu Farm's so delightful a home in which to live.'

16

Kirsty coloured a trifle at this, while her husband's expression revealed his pride.

'Yes,' responded Flint, picking up his glass from the table in front of him, 'you're quite right about Gimbulu Farm. It's a charming property.'

'But not in the same class as this,' Mark felt drawn to say, and Liane could not help but notice the sudden frown that touched Flint's brow. However, he put his glass to his mouth and drank, then leant back in his chair, his eyes on Liane again.

'So you find this part of our continent primitive, Miss Goulden?'

'It's so vastly different from anything I've ever known. Yes, I do find it primitive. After only three or four days I find myself becoming absorbed by the idea that here, in a land like this, one could live one's life much as nature ordained it to be lived.' So grave her tones; she was deep in thought and the swift astonished glances of Mark and Kirsty passed by unobserved.

'Away from the concrete blocks and television aerials, the turbulence of the highways and the massed complex of cubicles in which man—the most intelligent animal of them all—imprisons himself?' The question had a caustic ring but was yet seriously spoken. Liane, for the moment forgetful of the other two, looked at Flint and said,

'That's exactly what I mean, Mr Dawson. Where are we all going? Why have we removed ourselves from the freedom of wide open spaces like this and established ourselves in high-rise flats where even the air around us is befouled?' Her beautiful blue-green eyes were wide, and faintly tinged with shadow. Her mouth was not quite still, nor were her hands. Flint's gaze was fixed upon her face with a degree of interest that contrasted markedly with the cool impersonal polish of his first words of greeting. Liane, still forgetful of the other two, became vitally aware of Flint's intent examination of her features, as if he were committing to his memory every detail of her appearance.

'Where are we going?' His repetition of her question came at length, spoken in a quiet, thoughtful tone of voice. 'Man, Miss Goulden, is obsessed by the material things of life. To him, concrete and plastic represent these material things——'

'Oh, Flint,' protested Kirsty, who had plainly had enough of such sober and depressing observations, 'don't be so pessimistic! You'll be telling us next that man is rushing headlong towards his own destruction, for this appears to be the pronouncement one repeatedly hears from those pundits whom the ordinary, common people know only as "they" and "them".'

'He certainly rushes about,' intervened Mark, 'though it always seems to me that he's doing this in order to get himself more time for leisure——'

'It wasn't that kind of rushing about I meant,' said his wife, and Mark immediately nodded his head, saying he knew this.

'It was just something that came into my mind,' he ended, casting a glance towards Flint as if inviting some comment from him.

'Mark's right,' he said. 'This physical rushing about is indeed so that more time for leisure can be gained. But then what does man do with this leisure? He sits on a chair with his eyes glued to a television set.'

'When he could be out in the fresh air exploring the wide open spaces.' Mark shrugged his shoulders and

18

added with a hint of indifference, 'Why should we worry? We have the life we've chosen to live.'

'You're fortunate,' put in Liane, and there was no mistaking the hint of a sigh in her voice. 'People like me——' She spread her hands in a little helpless gesture. 'We have no choice but to live close to a town, because this is where we work.'

'Let's change the subject,' said Kirsty decisively. 'Flint, am I right in thinking that there'll be a dance at the Club next Saturday night?'

'Yes, a dinner dance. You'll be there?' Although his question was addressed to Kirsty his hooded eyes were on Liane. Kirsty said yes, they would all be there. She was watching Flint's expression, aware that he was again interested in her young cousin, and appearing to commit to memory each lovely detail of her appearance —the sweet-tempered mouth above a pointed, pixie-like chin, the large widely-spaced eyes, that, like the sea, could change from blue to green. They were framed by long dark lashes which at this moment were throwing adorable shadows on to her alabaster cheeks. Flint's eyes moved almost imperceptibly from Liane's high, clear forehead and delicate temples to the halo of russet hair, gleaming in the soft light which filtered through the canopy of vines from the lamp which was hidden within them. Again his eyes moved, to her mouth and throat and attractive curves and even to her small expressive hands with their long slender fingers and perfectly-shaped nails. Kirsty, aware of Flint's own impeccable taste in clothes, was in no doubt at all that he had noticed the dress which Liane had on, a dress which, like all her clothes, bore the mark of distinction and individuality.

'We must arrange some entertainments for Miss Goulden while she's here,' Flint decided at last. 'I myself shall be having one or two dinner parties, and perhaps a *braaivleis*.'

'That will be super!' smiled Kirsty. 'We shall have a dinner party too—and maybe a *braaivleis* as well.'

'And there'll be more dances at the Club, I suppose?' said Mark.

'Probably,' answered Flint thoughtfully. 'I believe Jim Berger's giving a party for his wife's birthday. If so we'll all be invited. It'll be a dinner dance or, perhaps, a dance and buffet.' His glance had strayed to Liane's glass, which was almost empty. 'Another drink?' he inquired with a smile. Liane sipped the last few drops of sherry and handed him the glass, saying she would have the same again.

'I don't really need all this entertainment,' she protested when once again the topic became centred on it. 'I love walking, and without a doubt there's a great deal to explore here. I'm content too when I'm wandering about the garden. I've been into Ravensville with Kirsty and I expect we shall be going again, many times. The hours will go all too quickly as it is.' This last sentence was accompanied by a glance of apology in Flint's direction. 'It's kind of you to think of me, but I'm very self-sufficient when it comes to keeping myself occupied.'

'You're an unusual person, Miss Goulden,' was Flint's unexpected response, and the hint of a smile touched his lips as he noticed the look of surprise which his words had produced on the faces of Kirsty and her husband.

'If you saw Flint's garden you'd not be so thrilled with wandering around ours,' said Kirsty after a space. 'It has the advantage of having been planned many years ago, and by an expert.'

'Yours will be just as mature one day,' returned Flint. And then he added, 'Miss Goulden, you must come over and see the gardens here. I have to agree with Kirsty that they're rather special—although I myself take no credit for their creation. As you've probably guessed, they were planted long before my time.'

Liane looked swiftly at him, wondering why she had been invited like this, to see the gardens of his home. Flint had struck her as friendly, but in a formal kind of way. That he would unbend sufficiently to invite her over to his house after little more than an hour in his company came as a surprise indeed.

'That's nice of you,' smiled Kirsty. 'Liane's free at any time.'

Liane coloured slightly at this eagerness on the part of her cousin. She was in no doubt as to the reason: Kirsty was anxious for Liane to have her days—and her mind—so completely occupied that there would be little or no chance of her brooding over the forthcoming marriage of the man she loved.

'In that case,' Flint was saying pleasantly, 'we'll make it tomorrow afternoon.'

Again Liane was taken aback, this time by the swift enthusiasm with which Flint had made the arrangements.

'Thank you very much,' she returned. 'It's kind of you to invite me over.'

The subject was changed, the dialogue becoming

casual, and for a few moments Liane permitted herself to withdraw from it and instead to relax in her chair and enjoy the lovely muted colours enveloping the landscape as dusk succumbed to the gentle invasion of night. The kopjes, ethereal in their folded tapestry of lavender and pearl, contrasted with the bushveld at their feet, where the last dying tints of gold and topaz had persistently remained, as if desiring to prolong the light of day. Drugged by the heady perfume of flowers carried on the breeze, she watched the painted sky change from amethyst to deep purple within a matter of minutes, heralding the darkness through which the stars would appear, garlanding the sky with argent points of light, and dappling the waters of the fountain and the pool in Flint's garden.

He was speaking, and Liane's attention was caught by the clear, attractive modulation of his voice. She turned her head and took a critical look at his face, an arresting face with dark saturnine features, the thrusting jaw depicting power and personality, the hard stern mouth, the grey, alert eyes, austere, incalculable at this moment, yet they had been lazy a few moments ago, made narrow by those heavy lids. He transferred his attention to her, attracted by her intense scrutiny. He smiled, a trifle quizzically, she thought, flushing at the idea of his perception in guessing that she had been making a very thorough examination of his features. His reaction to her scrutiny surprised her; she felt that an arrogant lifting of those straight dark eyebrows would be more characteristic of his noble and superior personality. But instead he merely stared at her—in a slightly disconcerting manner, it was true—as if waiting for her to speak. But it was Mark who broke the silence, plunging into a series of questions on the advisability of growing citrus fruits.

'It requires a good deal of thought,' said Flint after a few moments' consideration. 'Surely you're doing very well as you are—with mixed farming?'

'Yes, certainly, but I just had an urge to try something new.'

Flint nodded, then talked a little about the various aspects—and the hazards—of a change in one's farming methods and products. Kirsty, listening for a while, frowned at her husband and requested that the subject be changed. Flint laughed, surprising Liane, who would have expected *him* to frown, and to continue with the subject.

'Bored, are you, Kirsty? Mark, if you must discuss business then I'll come over within the next day or so and talk over possible changes with you.'

'Thanks, Flint. I'll value your advice.'

The evening was wearing on and eventually it was time for the visitors to be leaving. Flint walked with them to the gate, beneath a languorous moon, gigantic and pale in the midst of the crowded constellations.

The path narrowed; Kirsty and Mark went on ahead, and a little distance grew between them and the pair following, as Flint's pace was set slower than that of Mark.

'How peaceful it all is!' Carried away by everything around her—the dreamy sky, the soporific perfumes floating on the breeze, the silence and the purity of the bush through which a slow, primordial pulse-beat seemed to throb, Liane found herself whispering her

23

words. 'I've never known such quietness and—solemnity.'

He glanced down at her in the moonlight, commenting on her hesitation over the last word.

'You find the bushveld solemn, then?' he added, and Liane said yes, she did find the bushveld solemn, and awe-inspiring too.

'It's remote,' she added, almost to herself, for she was thinking of London and the press of people and buildings and traffic, the stifling lack of space and pure clean air. She looked upwards; the stars seemed low-hung now, and amazingly brilliant. 'It's magical,' she breathed, again almost to herself. She realised that the picture of London having brought back the memory of Richard and his engagement, she was now desperately striving to keep her mind on this present time, for here were peace and beauty, both of which could act as a balm to her hurt if only she were sensible enough to utilise them in this way.

'You sound as if you're a romantic, Miss Goulden.' A trace of amusement edged her companion's voice and Liane gave a little laugh and turned her head swiftly, so that the moonlight caught her hair as it swung against his arm. It shone and she noticed his eyes flicker to it, then to her face and her eyes.

'Anyone with a soul at all would find romance here,' she answered readily, but the next moment she had withdrawn and a flush had suffused her cheeks, for Flint had said, a most odd inflection in his tone,

'There are several kinds of romance, and I hope the one you have discovered will not be confined to that which you find in nature.'

Was he trying to flirt with her? She frowned and

24

shook her head. Flint Dawson did not in any way strike her as a man who would waste his time on such frivolities. Besides, he already had a girl-friend, Alma of the willowy figure and the husky voice.

# CHAPTER TWO

THE following afternoon Liane, looking extremely young and attractive in a sun-dress of turquoise linen trimmed with white piping on the neck, waist and hem, made her way to Kimara Lodge by the road approach, which was really a long avenue of coconut palms, beneath which smouldered the lovely crimson flowers of the oleanders, while beneath them again were the pretty waving heads of the brilliant yellow buttercups. On both sides of the road were Flint's citrus orchards, flourishing under the African sun. Farther away in the distance stretched the bushveld, and the colours typical of Africa—terracotta and honey-brown. Mountains rose in the far background, their heads wreathed in drifts of argent cloud, while lower down dark folds of shade gave a mysterious quality to the scene and Liane found herself conjuring up visions of past centuries, and the intangible unknown era when this beautiful country was uninvaded by the white man.

She sighed a little but could not have explained why. But the faint access of dejection was a sort of natural prelude to an influx of memories and before she realised it she was deep in thoughts of what might have been had she played her cards a little more cleverly where her relationship with her employer was concerned.

26

But, looking back, she had never, until the shock of the engagement, fully realised the depth of her secret love for the big, handsome business magnate with the cold eyes and impersonal tone of voice. Kirsty had guessed a long while previously; on questioning Liane directly she had received the truthful answer that her cousin was in love with her boss and that she cherished the hope that one day he would return that love. Kirsty, practical and far-seeing, had without hesitation told Liane to forget him, but Liane secretly admitted that although Kirsty spoke a good deal of sense, her wise counsel was far too difficult to follow.

Her reverie was suddenly brought to an end as Liane reached the high, filigreed gates through which she must pass on entering the grounds of Kimara Lodge. They opened noiselessly on well-oiled hinges; she closed them after her and stood for a few seconds taking a sweeping preview of the magnificent gardens. To her right was a lake of complicated shape, its winding shores fringed with trees. At one curving end stood a cluster of jacarandas, their blossoms hanging low like a soft blue veil of lace, while just a short distance away stood a rondavel, with vivid purple bougainvillaea tumbling over its thatched roof from an ornamental wall close by. Another vision of beauty which met Liane's appreciative and spellbound gaze was one of sweeping lawns and colour-spangled borders, of terraces and parterres beyond which an arched opening in a wall beckoned seductively and Liane wondered what treasures of nature lay beyond. She merely caught a glimpse of a delightful white rambler rose cascading over a trellis, its petals quivering like snowflakes in a breeze.

She walked on, along the well-kept drive bordered by flowers and low sweet-smelling shrubs. Taller trees met overhead, the sunlight sending darts of gold through their foliage to make dancing patterns on the ground.

She was almost at the front door when it opened and Flint's tall impressive form appeared, a half-smile on his sun-tanned face.

'Hello,' he greeted her, coming lightly down the flight of white marble steps. 'You look refreshingly cool. Doesn't our heat affect you at this time of the day?'

She nodded and said, in her quiet, musical voice,

'It does indeed. I had a cold shower just before I came out; that's why I appear to be cool.' She was at her ease, and yet, strangely, she was affected in some intangible way by the personality of the man—the air of supreme self-confidence and superiority, the faintly arrogant way in which he held himself, the noble lines of his face and the way his flint-like eyes could flicker with faint hauteur. She saw in one all-enveloping glance what he wore—the perfectly-cut slacks in dark blue linen, the white shirt, its collar immaculate against his copper-bronze throat, his gleaming sandals of off-white leather.

'You too look cool,' she said, returning his smile. 'But I expect that, being used to the excessive heat, you scarcely notice it?'

'That's partly correct. There are times, however, when even I can find it rather overpowering.' He flipped a hand, indicating the steps up to the shady stoep. 'You'll have a drink before we begin?'

'I'd love a fruit drink,' she returned. 'Orange if you have it?'

'Of course.' He saw her seated in one of the gay, cotton-covered leisure chairs, then went through into the room beyond and she heard the tinkle of glasses and ice. She leant back, crossing her legs and placing her hands on the arms of the chair, subconsciously aware that she was endeavouring to become totally relaxed and thought-free. But her yearning for Richard was there all the time, reminding her of her hopeless love for him. Could she go on working so close, knowing that he was married to another woman, that he would now leave the office each evening with a speed and eagerness not previously exhibited? She saw his home—so familiar because she had been there so many times, even having spent week-ends there if he had asked her to do so, on account of pressure of work. The house, standing in mature grounds of over two acres, was the typical example of the home of a prosperous business man. He had the highest quality carpets and curtains, the most expensive furniture. Antiques abounded and Liane had often visualised herself dusting these with loving care and aesthetic appreciation. The bedroom which Liane had occupied was lavishly fitted up, if a trifle cold in its decor. She had pictured herself subtly suggesting changes here and there about the house, bringing in her own character and, with it, warmth and colour.

Now all hope was gone, and suddenly a dark tide of despair pierced her mind and she wanted to abandon all restraint and find some small relief in tears. It would be so easy to weep——

'Your drink, Miss Goulden.' Flint's quiet voice came as a relief, putting an abrupt end to her melancholy thoughts, and she turned her head swiftly and produced a smile of thanks. The sunlight caught her hair, sending a ripple of gold through it, and Flint, his attention caught, stared for a moment, the most odd expression in his eyes. 'It's fresh orange juice,' he said presently. 'I'm not sure if you'll want some sugar?'

Liane took a drink, then shook her head.

'It's just right, thank you, Mr Dawson,' she smiled, watching him ease his long, sinewed body into the chair opposite to her. He held a glass of lemonade which he placed on the table in front of him.

'Do you mind if I call you Liane?' he asked after a pause. 'We don't often use surnames here, as you'll have already noticed, having been into town with Kirsty.'

'Yes, everyone she met called her by her Christian name.'

No more was said, but Liane knew that Flint had taken it for granted that he and she would now use Christian names when speaking to each other. They sat for about ten minutes, making light conversation, with Liane especially talking of trivial things—as people do when their hearts are breaking, she thought, memories once again surging in, poignant and futile.

Suddenly, unexpectedly, Flint said,

'Your eyes have a haunted look, Liane. What pictures are they seeing?'

'I—you——' She was so taken aback that she found herself lost for a reply. 'I didn't know I was looking any different from usual, Mr—er—Flint.'

A quirk of his lips betrayed his amusement at the small difficulty she had experienced in using his name for the first time.

'Come,' he said, easing the situation. 'Let me show

30

you around the gardens.' He stood up after making sure she had finished her drink. 'We'll begin at the front,' he decided, actually putting out a hand to assist her down the steps. 'First of all I shall show you my favourite place.'

It proved to be a little summer-house, thatched like the rondavel she had already seen, but this delightful little building, made of logs cut into the most intricate shapes which had been carefully fitted together, was set well back from the path among dark mango trees and other tropical vegetation.

'How lovely!' exclaimed Liane spontaneously, coming to a halt before the door, around which grew masses of crimson roses. 'If this were mine I'd come here very often!'

'I come here as often as I can,' Flint informed her. 'It's cool and shaded and lonely.'

'Lonely?' She lifted her head to look up into his lean tawny face. 'You want to be alone sometimes?'

'Of course,' he answered mildly. 'It's unnatural not to desire solitude now and then.'

'Solitude . . .' For a second time she repeated a word he had used, her eyes, as clear as blue Venetian glass, automatically wandering far beyond the precinct of the grounds of Kimara Lodge, to the wide bushlands which spread away to infinity, their burnt-umber colour shimmering in the heat-haze created by the fierce rays of the African sun. The scene was mystic and compelling, profound in its untamed isolation. 'There's plenty of solitude all around,' she murmured, speaking to herself. And then she said before he could comment on this, 'And in any case, you live alone.' The thought of his girl-friend intruded, along with the idea that Flint might not be living alone much longer.

'I live alone,' he agreed, but went on to point out that the domestic staff were always about. 'While at work I have many boys working with me,' he added. 'No, Liane, here and here alone can I be sure of remaining undisturbed.' He smiled down into her lovely face. 'Come inside,' he invited. 'You're privileged, my dear, because very few people are allowed to cross this threshold.'

My dear ...? Liane stared, quite unable to explain her feelings. A certain tenseness entered into her; she now seriously asked herself if Flint was the kind of man who would waste his time in so trivial a pastime as a flirtation. He was certainly far more friendly than she had expected him to be. From what Kirsty had said, Liane had formed a picture of cool impersonality, of aloofness and even indifference. Flint's attitude was far removed from this image, and in some vague way she felt she must be on her guard.

She entered the summer-house and gasped as she looked around. The floor was exquisitely tiled, with coconut matting in the centre. A couch in brightly-coloured linen matched the eggshell-blue curtains, while the walls, which had been plastered, were colour-washed in white. Small, well-chosen items of furniture and a couple of beautiful African wood carvings completed the picture, except for an inlaid bookcase containing several leather-bound volumes which, Liane surmised, were not usually kept in the summer-house because of probable damage by insects.

'It's beautiful.' She turned to him, noted that his interest was entirely with her and not with the room, and she felt her colour rise a little. 'Er—shall we go now?' Somehow, she wanted to be out in the open again, away from the isolation of the summer-house.

'Don't you want to sit down for a moment or two?'

She shook her head immediately.

'I'd rather look around the gardens,' she said.

He shrugged his broad shoulders. She sensed a tingle of disappointment in his demeanour but he did not press her to remain. Instead, he guided her towards a terrace where brilliant colour flared from the canna lilies and anthuriums, the bird of paradise flowers and the orange cliveas.

From there he showed her the borders, pointing out the varying colours of the hibiscus, the beauty of the Judas trees which looked like a violet haze when they were in bloom. There were the frangipanis which, he told her, were used so much in places like Bali for decorating temples: there were flamboyants and African tulip trees. He told her which were natives of the country and which had been imported; she learned that he had brought plants from many parts of the world, and his parents and grandparents before him had brought even more.

'No wonder it's such a beautiful garden,' she breathed when at last they were back on the stoep, once again with cool drinks in front of them. 'I've loved every moment of this afternoon, Flint. Thank you very much. It'll be a wonderful memory to take home with me.'

There was an instant vacuum of silence, startling her in its indefinable quality. Flint's face was a mask, taut and unreadable.

'You've a long time to go before you'll be thinking of going home.' He picked up his glass and, moving it, listened to the tinkle of ice against its side. 'You haven't been here a week yet.'

'No, but time passes swiftly when you're on holiday.' Liane had no idea why she should say this, for there was nothing she wanted more than for the time to pass slowly. The very idea of returning to the office, and working with Richard, aware that he was in love with another woman, was something from which she wanted to run away. Her face clouded, because of her thoughts, and her eyes withdrew from her surroundings into the painful memory; to the man sitting opposite to her she seemed to become lost in a shadow-dimmed realm of her own. He frowned and his voice was knife-sharp when he spoke.

'Your eyes have that haunted look again! What's wrong?' So imperious his tone, so authoritative his whole manner with her that she just stared, a strange tension gripping her like a vice.

'I don't know what you mean?' she prevaricated, and actually heard the swift impatient intake of Flint's breath.

'You're troubled over something,' he stated, his grey eyes fixing hers as if he would, by sheer hypnotism, force her to confide in him.

'I must confess that's the truth,' she decided to say. But she added, in a firm decisive tone of voice, 'However, it happens to be a matter which is so private that I can't talk about it.'

'I see.' His eyes were still intently focused on Liane's face as he added, 'You're young to have troubles. How old are you?'

Again she stared, this time at the bluntness of his query. Nevertheless, she told him her age, and saw him raise his dark eyebrows in surprise.

'Twenty-five?' His glance roved her figure and she averted her head. 'You look no more than twenty.' Liane coloured at his flattery but made no comment. 'With a face and figure like yours,' he said with the same lack of restraint as before, 'you should have been married long ago.' Flint's voice took on a peculiar inflection as the last few words left his lips, and Liane, flashing him a glance, saw that a slight frown had settled on his forehead.

'I shall never marry,' she told him, speaking automatically, revealing what was in her mind without stoping to think.

'Never marry?' repeated Flint, his voice sharpening again. 'That's a strange statement to make. Have you some strong aversion to marriage?'

Liane hesitated, wondering what to say in reply to this—and wondering also how it was that she had allowed the conversation to proceed along lines which were so disconcerting for her.

'I haven't an aversion in the way you are implying,' she began at last, and Flint's response was instantaneous.

'What am I implying, Liane?' Was there a quirk of amusement in his glance? If so, it was not reflected in the tones he used, for these were both serious and inquiring.

'I feel you were thinking that I was averse to men generally—except as friends and acquaintances, I mean.' She was embarrassed and it showed. Her slender fingers played uneasily with the glass she held, moving across its rim or tapping its side. Flint, watching her with an intentness that only added to her discomfiture, spoke at last, an unfathomable inflection in his tone.

'This statement that you will never marry? Am I correct in assuming it to be connected in some way with the trouble you've just mentioned?' He was pre-occupied all at once and Liane felt convinced he was endeavouring to make an intelligent guess as to what that 'trouble' was. And, noting his changing expression, she would not have been at all surprised had he asked outright if she were in love with a man who was un-attainable. She hesitated, searching her mind for some answer that would put him off the scent without her actually having to tell an untruth. She found none, and as Flint appeared to be determined to have an answer to his question she was forced to say,

'Yes, you are correct in your assumption that my decision never to marry is connected with the trouble I mentioned.'

Flint made no comment on this, but she sensed his continued preoccupation and when at length she said it was time she was leaving he nodded automatically as if he had scarcely taken in what she was saying.

He accompanied her all the way back to Gimbulu Farm, leaving her at the gate and saying he would be seeing her at the Club dance on Saturday evening.

Kirsty, who had watched from the living-room win-dow as Flint and Liane had strolled together up the road and then stood for a few moments by the gate, looked a little questioningly at her cousin as she en-tered the bright room that led off the stoep.

'I had a marvellous time!' Liane said, taking pos-session of a chair. 'Flint's gardens are really something! I've never seen such a wonderful array of colour and beauty.'

'They are delightful, as you say.' Kirsty had been arranging some tuberoses in a vase on a stink-wood table and she bent to continue with her task. 'Flint ...' She spoke slowly, and a little wonderingly. 'You and he are on Christian name terms already?'

'He said people always use first names here.'

'We who live here do, but I've never known Flint to be so eager to make friends with a stranger before. With people he doesn't know really well he seems to maintain a distance and aloofness that precludes any attempts at familiarity.' Kirsty straightened up to make a critical survey of her handiwork. 'Did he say anything about the dance on Saturday?'

'Only that he'd see me there.' Liane, though answering non-committally, was in her own mind pondering her cousin's words, which were pointed and at the same time puzzled. It was clear that Kirsty was a little baffled by Flint's attitude towards Liane.

'Alma will be at the dance.' Kirsty inhaled audibly, taking in the sweet scent of the tuberoses. 'Do you like my flower arrangement?' she asked, changing the subject.

Liane nodded, and smiled her appreciation.

'It's lovely—but you always were good at anything artistic. I've recently framed that embroidery you gave me. It's now on the wall in my bedroom.'

A silence followed, Kirsty making slight alterations to her flower arrangement and Liane staring through the open window to the tranquil, sun-caressed tableau beyond the boundary of the garden. To the west lay the undulating grassy slopes which formed part of Mark's pastureland, while to the east, shimmering like crystal in the refracted glare of the sun, lay the soft

37

dreamy bushveld, enfolded in peace. Ahead rose the mountains, their serrated ridges razor-sharp against the sky; their lower slopes, tree-clad, were often indistinct in contrast, shaded as they were by jutting outcrops forming barriers against the light.

'I suppose,' murmured Kirsty, bringing Liane's attention from the view outside, 'that I should be going to see what Sylvester's doing. We're having a roast this evening. I hope you'll not mind?'

'Mind?' blinked Liane. 'I shall love it!'

'The weather's more for salads, but to be honest, I'm becoming tired of them and I'm sure Mark is as well, though he never complains about anything that's set before him—the angel!' As always Kirsty's eyes glowed when she spoke of her husband; and Liane, watching her, knew a terrible emptiness inside, and a yearning for what might have been. She supposed it was the dream of every woman to have a husband, and a home where her children could be happy and secure. This dream had faded for Liane on that dark day when Richard had told her of his engagement to Marlene.

'Can I do anything to help with the dinner?' she asked suddenly, desirous of occupying her mind with something else. 'I'll see to the table if you like?'

'Thanks, Liane. I'll go and see what's cooking!' Grinning at her own joke, Kirsty went off to the kitchen, while Liane proceeded to the small dining-room whose large picture window looked out on to the western aspect of the gardens and the serene landscape beyond.

She had set the table and was back in the living-room when, hearing the runabout scrape to a halt outside, she glanced through the window to see Mark easing himself from the driver's seat. He had been into Ravensville to pick up some fertilisers he had ordered, and he had also done a little shopping for Kirsty at the same time.

'I met the Van der Galts,' he told his wife as she emerged from the kitchen. 'They've invited us over for dinner a week on Friday. There'll be about eight guests altogether, they said.'

'That'll be nice.' Kirsty looked at her cousin. 'For you, most probably. You'll like the Van der Galts; they're farmers, like us, and have a son and daughter helping them. Kathie's twenty and Carl's twenty-six.'

'You mean they're giving the dinner party just because I'm here?' Liane looked amazed. 'I've never known such hospitality!'

'We all want you to carry away happy memories when you leave us.' Mark, looking a little hot and unkempt from his dusty drive up from Ravensville, smiled at Liane, his keen brown eyes seeming to be looking for some sign that her heartache was lightening. Liane had not wanted Kirsty to let Mark know of her foolishness in falling in love with her boss, but she supposed it had been too much for Kirsty to keep it to herself. However, Mark seemed far more sympathetic than amused and Liane had not suffered the smallest degree of embarrassment because of his being in possession of the knowledge of her unrequited love for her employer.

'I don't want to think of leaving,' she confessed with a sudden frown. 'I could settle here, in fact.'

'Then why don't you?' encouraged Kirsty. 'With your experience you could soon get yourself a job in Ravensville.'

Liane sighed and shook her head.

'It would be too much of a risk, Kirsty. I'd have to sell up everything I have——'

'No such thing! You can bring all your furniture here.'

Liane said nothing to this suggestion. She was thinking of Richard and his reliance on her. She could not desert him, she decided, her swift-winged thoughts bringing back those words he had uttered when she had been leaving the office to begin her holiday.

'I must confess, Liane, I shall be happy indeed on the day you return to the office.'

No, she could not desert him. Always she would be there, on hand, if ever he should really need her.

# CHAPTER THREE

LIANE'S dress whirled as she danced, gossamer light, in Flint's arms. The dress was of ivory organza, tight at the waist, with a bouffant skirt, the hemline of which was scalloped. On each scallop was an embroidered rose, pink alternating with apricot, all the way round. Behind each rose were two small leaves of vivid green. The long sleeves, tightly drawn in at the wrists, began their fullness at the waistline of the dress, and hung in numerous delicate folds. The neckline was high, trimmed with tiny scallops on which were embroidered roses matching those on the hem. There had been gasps when Liane had entered the lobby of the Club, and every head had turned. Previously, Kirsty had gone into raptures over the dress, and stated emphatically that she herself intended to 'get in on this dress sense lark' and that Liane would be made to help her.

'There'll not be a dress to come up to this one!' she had declared, and she was right.

'Liane ...' Flint's voice had faded almost at once; he had seemed totally lost for something to say. Liane, flushing delicately, had lifted her clear blue eyes to his ... and she had wished the admiration she found there had been in the eyes of the man she loved. 'How exquisite!' Something else followed the exclamation,

41

something that sounded like, 'She might have stepped out of a Goya canvas,' but the voice had dropped so low that Liane could not be sure. He had been like a person hypnotised, unable to take his eyes from her. His inordinate appreciation was so plain for Liane to see, yet she derived no special pleasure from it, for her thoughts were far away, with a big, broad-shouldered businessman, and it was his admiration which she craved.

As Mark and Kirsty were called away by two young friends of theirs, Flint took Liane off to the terrace, where they sat with their drinks, both silent—Flint thoughtful and Liane idly watching the moths and beetles flying round the lamps. Earlier, an enormous moon had risen over the horizon and it was now high in the sky, shedding its silver glow across the soft grey skein of the bushveld.

At last Flint broke the silence, inviting Liane to dance. Smilingly she accepted, and even though her thoughts were with another man, she could not help feeling a tinge of pride at finding herself the partner of a man as handsome and arresting as Flint.

'You dance exceedingly well.' His voice, soft and finely-timbred, caused Liane to glance up, giving him a charming smile.

'Thank you, Flint.' Her voice was neither warm nor cool. She did not take his praise for granted, but neither could she give him cause to assume that she was in any way affected by it.

'You're a very charming young lady,' he said, his arm about her tightening a little.

'Thank you,' she said again, her voice detached, as before. She was thoroughly enjoying the dance; she was

—womanlike—thrilled with her appearance, aware, without being in any way immodest, that she was the most tastefully dressed female present. This knowledge brought her interest to her partner, and she was soon admitting that he was the best-dressed, most distinguished-looking male present. Clad in a white dinner jacket which had been superbly cut, he seemed to stand out as a model of perfection. Suddenly Liane smiled, thinking that Flint would dislike excessively the description she had mentally given to him.

'Amused about something?' Smooth the voice now, and it dawned upon her all at once that he might be a little piqued at her total lack of response to his flattery.

'I was amused, yes,' she replied, incurably honest.

'Might I share the joke?' His bronzed face was bent to hers; his flint-like eyes were questioning.

'It wasn't a joke, exactly. I was merely amused by my reflections.'

He seemed to give a slight sigh, but made no comment and they danced in silence until the music stopped.

A few introductions were made then, as many more people had arrived. Liane met the Van der Galts—Frederick and his wife Marthe, and their two children, Carl and Kathleen. She also met Sam and Maisie, the young friends of Mark and Kirsty. And she met Alma.

The girl would be sure to arrive late, Kirsty had told Liane.

'She likes to make a dramatic entrance at the end of a dance when everyone has the opportunity of looking at her.'

Kirsty was right; Alma did arrive late, just as a dance finished and everyone was coming off the floor. She stood in the high arched opening which separated the lounge from the ballroom, her svelte figure clad in black velvet trimmed with sparkling Lurex, her sleek head of dark brown hair set a little to one side—an affectation, declared Kirsty later in a voice of contempt. The eyes, of the unusual colour of olivine, and as hard, were faintly narrowed beneath the level brows as they made a sweeping survey of the faces which were turned towards her. A smile touched her lips as she caught sight of Flint, and she glided towards the small group of people with whom he was chatting. The introduction took place; the green eyes kindled strangely as they looked into Liane's beautiful face. Then they ran over her figure, taking in the elegance of her dress, and its beautifully detailed ornamentation of exquisitely embroidered roses. As the girl continued to take unhurried stock of her, Liane felt her temper rise. She glanced at Flint, saw the suspicion of a smile upon his firm mouth and wondered what he was thinking. More than this, however, she wondered what he saw in this tall slender girl with the swaying hips and narrow shoulders, and that deep and husky voice with which she was now commenting,

'I'm late again, Flint. It was Letsie's fault! She took ages doing my hair.'

Letsie, Kirsty later told Liane, was the coloured maid-of-all-work who did everything for Alma from her washing and ironing to running her bath water and shampooing and setting her hair.

'She made an excellent job of it, nevertheless,' smiled Flint, allowing his eyes to wander over Alma's immaculate head before transferring his attention to her dress—slashed low back and front—and then, un-

44

expectedly, to Liane's. He seemed to be mentally comparing the two outfits; Alma's mouth tightened as she watched him, and she swallowed hard, as if anger had affected her throat.

Mark asked Liane to dance and within a few minutes Flint and Alma were on the floor, two tall people moving in perfect harmony, both possessing a high degree of self-confidence, both carrying a measure of arrogance and pomposity.

'What do you think of Flint's girl-friend?' Kirsty was asking a short while later when she joined Liane and Mark as they came off the floor when the music stopped.

'Not my type,' was Liane's frank admission. 'Too worldly, and sophisticated.' Her thoughts flashed to Marlene, who had been so successful in winning Richard's love. She was of the same type as Alma, self-confident, sophisticated. 'However, women like Alma seem to appeal to the men,' she added with an apologetic glance at Mark.

He laughed and assured her that Alma's type would never in a hundred years appeal to him.

'Nor do I honestly believe she appeals to Flint,' he added with a glance in the direction of the bar, where Flint and Alma were now standing, glasses in their hands. 'She throws herself at him and I expect he finds this both flattering and diverting. But it's my opinion that she wouldn't have a cat in the hot shop's chance if it came to marriage. Flint'll eventually choose a nice, timid little girl who'll do as she's told.'

'You mean,' said Liane with an amused smile, 'that she'll have no will of her own?' Her eyes moved to Flint's tall figure. His profile was towards her, its lines

45

severe, implacable. Kirsty had said, when first describing him to Liane,

'He's a man accustomed to asserting his authority. With his boys—the Africans who work for him on his estate—he wields that authority without either effort or unnecessary forcefulness. But they know he'll not stand any nonsense and they act accordingly.'

'She'll have precious little will of her own,' Mark was saying in answer to Liane's question. 'There isn't much doubt about who'll be the boss in Flint's house.'

'He has a scathing tongue at times,' submitted Kirsty with a grimace. 'He once had a go at me, because I thought fit to suggest that Mark was doing something wrong on the farm.'

Mark nodded and laughed.

'You said I ought to have experimented with a cotton crop.'

'Ah, yes, I remember now. I'd forgotten what it was I'd done wrong. Flint advised Mark against it and when I argued with him he gave me the telling off of my life.'

No more was said, for at this moment Flint came across to say that dinner was being served and that they were to sit with him and Alma.

'Carl Van der Galt's making up the third man,' he added, his eyes meeting Liane's with an intense stare. 'I've arranged for us to have a table near the window, so we shan't be lacking fresh air.'

The window was wide open, and led to a verandah. Outside all was still, with a clear pale moon riding the high-flung sky, a deep purple sky spangled with stars. The perfume of flowers hung on the air, and from the trees came the ceaseless trilling of the cicadas.

It was a magic evening, possessing a sort of pagan splendour.

'Sit here, opposite to me.' Flint's voice brought Liane's attention from the beauty of the moonlit scene to the chair he was indicating, and she sat down. Alma, a quality of tautness about her, raked Liane's figure then turned away, as if she had seen more than enough.

'She's always stolen the show before,' Kirsty was whispering when they were all seated to Flint's satisfaction. 'But tonight she looks positively shabby beside you——'

'Kirsty, please!' whispered Liane, blushing.

'I'm only stating a fact,' persisted Kirsty, unrepentant. 'That slinky, sexy dress she's wearing doesn't do a thing for her, although she obviously believes it does.'

'Mark and Kirsty, what wine are you drinking?' Flint was ordering and he waited while Mark glanced down the wine list. Alma was sitting back in her chair, a certain languor about her even though her eyes, now fixed on Liane, were alert. Aware of her stare, Liane met her gaze, automatically tilting her head a little in an unconscious protest against the girl's rudeness. Once again Alma turned away, this time to speak to Flint, producing an alluring smile as she did so. Liane heard her reminding Flint that he was dining with her and her parents on the following Wednesday, but that he would be welcome to go over on the Monday for a sundowner. Kirsty, deeply interested in the interchange taking place between Alma and Flint, glanced several times in Liane's direction. Liane was sitting there, an expression of indifference on her face. But soon she was chatting with Carl, whom she had liked in the way

47

she had liked Mark, finding an attractiveness in his charming manner and spontaneity. He was open and frank, with dark blue honest eyes and light brown hair which was thick and wiry and clinging low on his forehead. He had a gaiety about him which proclaimed him to be trouble-free and contented with his lot.

Between courses the three couples danced, and Liane was soon left in no doubt about Carl's growing admiration for her. She danced like an angel, he told her, to which she laughingly responded,

'How do you know? Have you ever danced with an angel?'

Carl laughed with her and at that moment they happened to come close to Flint and Alma. Alma was staring dreamily up into her partner's face, but Flint, for some incomprehensible reason, seemed to be oblivious of the girl's attention, his face set and preoccupied.

'Darling,' Liane heard Alma say in tones both silky and complaining, 'you're miles away!'

He looked down into her eyes and his lips moved. Liane failed to catch his words, as Carl guided her deftly through the dancers, back to their table, which they occupied alone for a few moments until joined by the other four as the music stopped.

'Would you be offended—or embarrassed—if I compliment you on your appearance?' He gave her no opportunity of answering as he added, his blue eyes flicking over her face and neck and down to her hands, one of which was holding a glass, 'You're the most attractive woman here this evening——'

'Please!' She spoke rather more sharply than she intended but she *was* embarrassed, aware of the colour rising in her cheeks. 'I'd rather talk about something else. Tell me about your farm. What do you grow? And how do you market your produce?'

Faintly he smiled, discouraged by her first sharp exclamation.

'You're not really interested, Liane,' he said slowly and with resignation. 'In any case, here come the others.'

The meal progressed amid light chatter, subjects being introduced, exhausted, then followed by others. Carl was faintly subdued and Liane was sorry about this, chiding herself for adopting that abrupt manner; she could have been more gentle in her tones of protest. Kirsty and Mark were, as usual, full of exuberance; Alma was effusive one moment and elaborately casual the next. Flint was the listener, commenting now and then but for the most part attending with silent interest to what the others were saying. As for Liane, she was vaguely conscious of a tension in the air; it was something indefinable, yet troublesome. No one else appeared to be affected by it and in the end she concluded it was her imagination which was causing this strange sensation of tenseness.

Flint danced mainly with Alma, but he naturally danced with Kirsty and Liane, in addition to one or two others present.

'How are you enjoying your first Club dinner dance?' His voice was casual and light as he put the question to Liane as he held her lissom body in his arms as they danced a waltz, long after the meal was finished.

'I'm enjoying it very much.' Her eyes were bright, her mouth slightly parted as a smile hovered enchantingly on her lips. 'I had no idea it would be like this.'

'What—the building itself or the atmosphere?'

49

'Both. The people are so friendly—they actually seem thrilled at the idea of meeting a foreigner.'

'We welcome strangers,' he said. 'I expect it's because we have so few of them. When one of us is expecting a visitor from a distance it becomes news as soon as we mention it. Everyone knew that Kirsty was expecting a visit from her cousin in England.'

'Do you have visitors?'

'I've a few relatives who come to me now and then. One, an aged aunt, will be here in a couple of weeks' time. You'll like her; she considers marriage as the greatest folly a woman can commit.'

Liane laughed, but it was a forced laugh, and this did not escape her partner, who leant away and looked down into her face.

'How old is she?' Liane wanted to know, pretending she had not noticed the odd expression on Flint's countenance.

'Eighty-one three days after she arrives. I always find myself having to give her a party.'

'Eighty-one! And she still travels by herself?'

'Of course. She'll still be with us when she's a hundred.'

Liane fell silent, thinking of Flint and his complex personality. Kirsty had declared that he could have a scathing tongue at times; Mark had implied that he was the type who would domineer over his wife. Yet she, Liane, had seen very little she did not like, and now he was mildly accepting the visit from his aged aunt, who obviously did not have much time for his sex, and resignedly telling Liane that he would be expected to give a party for her.

'I shall look forward to seeing her ...' Liane's voice

50

trailed away as she realised that she was being gently and subtly propelled towards the open french window of the ballroom. 'Where are we going?'

'Don't you find it a little overpowering in here?'

'Well ... er——'

'You do? I thought you would. A stroll in the gardens will refresh you——'

'I didn't say I was in need of fresh air,' she told him severely. 'I see no necessity at all for wandering out there, in the dark.'

'Very romantic,' he laughed, and calmly took her elbow and almost pushed her the last few feet towards the window. 'African nights always are romantic.'

She was nonplussed, thinking of Alma and surmising that the girl would be far from pleased if she had seen what was happening. When last Liane saw her she was dancing with Carl, and not looking any too happy about it.

The air outside was clear and fresh, and tinged with flower scents hovering on the zephyr of a breeze. Flint, tall and distinguished as he walked beside Liane, seemed pensively withdrawn, and her puzzlement grew. He was in a strange unfathomable mood which she would not have associated with a man as coolly aloof as Flint. It was almost as if he were unsure of himself!

'Is that lovely dress catching on the ground?' he asked suddenly, as if he were concerned about the dress now that he had remembered the sort of ground over which they were walking.

'No, I'm holding it up.'

'Good. It's far too delicate and attractive to be spoiled.'

Liane glanced up at him but was silent, his mood

51

still occupying her thoughts as she tried to analyse it.

She stood still as they reached a place where the path turned, into a thicket of bushes, and listened to the drilling note of the cicadas.

'They still fascinate me,' she said, speaking her thoughts aloud. 'The cicadas, I mean,' she added for his benefit.

'You've never heard them before coming here?'

Liane shook her head, glancing upwards swiftly as something flew above her head—a bat or a night bird, she surmised.

'No, I haven't. There must be millions of them.'

'I expect there are.' He was looking down into her face, an odd expression in his grey eyes. 'What else do you find fascinating about Africa?'

'Many things,' she replied at once. 'The lovely sunshine and warmth, the landscape generally, which is so different from ours at home. I love also the silence and the impression of mystery and antiquity.'

'You're a strange girl, Liane,' he said unexpectedly.

'Strange?' Liane glanced over the dark immensity of the veld till her eyes met the mountains, gaunt in the moonlight. 'I don't understand?'

'You're deep ... very deep.'

She turned her head, frowning up at him.

'That's not a very flattering thing to say to me!'

'Sorry!' Flint laughed briefly. 'I didn't mean it in the way you've taken it. I meant that I wish I could fathom what's going on in that quiet mind of yours.'

'Our thoughts are the one thing we can be sure of keeping to ourselves.'

He nodded his head and for a space there was silence except for the cicadas.

'Tell me,' he said at last, 'how do you come to have six weeks' holiday? It isn't usual, I think?'

'I had some weeks owing to me from last year.' Walking on again, Liane was aware that the action stemmed from a desire to discourage any further questions from her companion, but she failed.

'You mean you didn't have any holidays last year?'

'I had a few days.' She spoke casually, idly extending a hand to caress the delicate foliage of a bush as she passed it. 'I didn't mind not taking my holidays,' she added, suspecting that Flint was about to put another question to her.

'It seems odd to me.' He was frowning slightly as she lifted her head to glance up into his face. She had the impression that he wanted to know a great deal more about her job, and her life in general. Strange ... Why should the aloof and superior Flint Dawson be taking so much interest in her? Liane was asking herself this again a few minutes later when, after she had successfully changed the subject, Flint said suddenly,

'I've noticed that you avoid answering questions about yourself. It's an attitude I've never before found in a woman. You usually like talking about yourselves.' There was the merest hint of amusement in his tone, but the underlying meaning was pointed and clear. Liane paused, certain that this behaviour was far removed from what was customary with him.

'I suppose I feel that my affairs are private,' she decided to say, hoping that he would take the hint and refrain from pressing her for information which she felt unwilling to give.

'Withdrawing into yourself ...' Flint's voice, though

resonant, was low, and his manner was one of pre-occupation. Liane felt that he was puzzled by her reticence, for, as he had just implied, women were not usually averse to talking about themselves.

She said, making her voice light and friendly,

'Shall we go back?'

Flint glanced down at her, his brows raised at the way she had ignored his comment, and a momentary embarrassment seized her. But this was suddenly replaced by indignation as into her mind was thrust the question: what right had Flint to raise his eyebrows in censure simply because she had not wanted to become involved in a conversation about herself? Aware that her avoidance was due to the ever-present image of Richard, she became fiercely resentful of Flint's company, resentful that it was he who was strolling by her side in this romantic setting ... he and not Richard.

Tears gathered behind her eyes, and she caught her underlip between her teeth. She knew for sure that, should Flint notice a dampness appear on her lashes, he would instantly demand to know the reason for it.

'Do you want to go back?' he inquired at last in response to her suggestion. 'We haven't been out for more than five minutes or so.'

There was a short pause as Liane found herself in a state of indecision. Much to her surprise she was not really eager to leave the tranquillity of the Club grounds and return to the lights and noise of the ballroom.

'We can stay out for another few minutes if you wish,' she said. 'It's certainly cool and quiet here, in the grounds.' They were approaching an avenue of

54

blue gums beyond which all appeared to be dark, and very lonely, remote as it was from the lights of the Club building. 'Do you want to go this way?' She frowned even as she spoke, aware that her mind was confused; she ought not to go into the dark and lonely places ... and yet something seemed to draw her and she found herself lifting her dress a little higher, as if in a precautionary measure against damage.

'Yes, we'll go this way.' Flint's tone was casual as he added, 'You'd better let me guide you, Liane. The path's uneven in places. They don't seem to take much interest in this part of the gardens.'

He soon took her arm; she knew no emotion whatever at the contact, but her thoughts flew to Richard, and a terrible yearning swept over her. If only this were Richard ...

Flint spoke, breaking into her thoughts and she looked up in the darkness, glad of the interruption and yet, paradoxically, resenting it. For this was a moment when she actually wanted to think of Richard, wanted to invent a scene of intimacy between herself and him ... a scene where she was being taken into his arms, in this dark and silent place.

'Be careful where you tread, Liane. If I remember correctly there are some small boulders just hereabouts.' She kept his warning in mind, but in spite of this Liane did step on a boulder and was flung against Flint's tough and sinewed body. His other arm came out instantly and supported her, and for a few seconds he held her close. She felt his cool clean breath on her cheek before she drew away, giving a little gasp before expressing her thanks.

'I'd have gone headlong,' she added. 'Perhaps we ought to turn back.'

'There's a delightful little waterfall just outside the Club grounds,' he told her. 'It's in a wooded glade and is in reality a spring. You'll be enchanted with it.'

'It's outside the grounds?' Liane was still close to him; his hand was still placed protectingly beneath her elbow.

'Yes; there's a gate at the end of these trees which leads to the wooded glade I mentioned.' Already he was moving on and Liane made no protest, but fell into step beside him until the end of the avenue was reached and Flint unfastened the gate so that they could pass through.

The glade, she thought, was like a green fairyland, its waterfall plainly visible in the light of a full moon shining from a cloudless sky. The night was warm and sleepy, the landscape fringed with starlight. Glancing up involuntarily, Liane recognised Sagittarius and Scorpio, and the Southern Triangle. Arching above was the Milky Way, a luminous band streaking across the deep purple dome of the sky. Noises assailed her ears—the silver-toned cascading of the water over the rocks, the rustle of leaves disturbed by the breeze, the flutter of wings and the nervous cry of a monkey disturbed, the incessant rhythm of cicadas sharpening their wings.

Beyond and above these sounds there reigned a great and awe-inspiring silence—the lonely silence of the African bush.

'Well ...?' Flint's voice intruded into Liane's appreciative study of her surroundings and she lifted her head, producing a ready smile. 'What do you think of this little glade?'

'It's ... beautiful ... and magical.' Her breath caught and held. She felt as if she had drunk of a heady wine, so intoxicating was the effect upon her—not only of the glade itself, but of the atmosphere in general. It was unreal, something conceived by a maker of magic. Liane's senses were pleasantly lulled; Richard seemed never to have existed. She could not bring his face into focus, and she had no desire to do so. 'I imagine that heaven must be something like this,' she murmured at length, speaking to herself rather than to her companion.

Flint laughed and it seemed that a great happiness had spread over him.

'I'm glad you like it.' He paused then, and as on a previous occasion, she had the impression that he was unsure of himself. But if this were so he soon recovered, for his voice rang with the confidence which by now was familiar to Liane. 'From now on it will be "Liane's Glade".'

'My——?' She glanced up again, searching his face. 'I don't understand?'

'The land hereabouts belongs to me,' he told her, adopting a casual tone of voice. 'I'm offering this to you, as a gift. I hope that you will accept it, Liane.' So sincere the offer, and the tone of delivery. Liane, suddenly filled with emotion, felt she could not be so churlish as to refuse, even though it flashed through her mind, quite naturally, that the gift would never really do her any good. Long afterwards she would ask herself why she accepted—what force controlled her thoughts and reaction that resulted in her saying,

57

'How very wonderful of you, Flint! Is this enchanting place really to be mine?'

'It's yours, my dear—from this very moment.'

She said, in quiet tones,

'Thank you, Flint. I shall love to own this tiny bit of Africa.' Then, after a thoughtful moment, she just had to add, 'I shall probably never see it, though, when once I've left here in five weeks' time.'

A silence followed, broken only by the sound of running water as the cascade fell from its height among the rocks into the pool below. Liane sensed a taut unfathomable quality about her companion, yet for herself there was only peace, and a strange contentment which she would never have believed possible when first she had made her decision to come out to Africa for this holiday. She stood by the pool, her eyes fixed on the silver stream as it flowed, ribbon-like, from its source in a fissure in the rocks. And she thought that she could quite easily live here, in this primitive part of the continent, among people whose ideas of perfect living were those of staying as close to nature as was possible.

'I suppose,' Flint was saying, though reluctantly, 'we ought to be returning to our friends.'

Liane nodded in the moonlight.

'We've been out ages.' Was he thinking of Alma, and wanting to be back with her? Suddenly Alma was as unimportant as Richard, for it was as if Liane and Flint were quite alone in this realm which was so hauntingly still and peaceful. He moved and it seemed that he was in a restless mood. His eyes as they met hers had a piercing quality in their regard. Right out of the blue he said,

'This idea of yours against marriage. Do you honestly mean that you prefer the path of loneliness? Do you live the life of a hermit at home?'

Liane frowned in amazement at the unexpectedness of the questions, questions for which she saw no logical reason.

'I don't live like a hermit,' she replied after a pause. 'On the other hand, I don't go out very much. My job has always been demanding; it takes up most of my time.'

It was Flint's turn to frown.

'By your job you mean of course your boss. It's he who is demanding? Or do you work for a woman?'

She coloured slightly, and turned her face away from his gaze.

'I work for a man,' she answered briefly.

'Tell me about your work.' Imperious the tone all at once and his manner was, to say the least, proprietorial.

Mystified, Liane found herself weakening beneath this strong but inexplicable attitude, and her resolve not to talk about herself was forgotten as, beginning to answer his question, she carried on speaking until she had given Flint a fairly comprehensive picture of the life she led at home.

She had no idea that, unconsciously, she had betrayed all that she felt for the big, handsome man for whom she worked.

Several seconds passed before Flint spoke.

'This Richard's just become engaged to be married, you said?'

Lianne nodded, adopting an air of indifference.

'Yes; he told me about it a short time before I de-

59

cided to accept Kirsty's invitation and come out here for a holiday.'

Flint was nodding thoughtfully, and his mouth was inexplicably grim.

'Let's go back,' he said abruptly. 'As you say, we've been out for a long time.' He began to walk away from the pool by which they had been standing; Liane followed and he paused so that she could fall into step beside him. A tension had come down—like a cloud, she thought, wondering at the change in Flint, who now seemed so grim and formidable that Kirsty's original description of him fitted perfectly.

Soon they were through the gate and proceeding along the avenue of blue gums. Liane did not expect Flint to display the concern which he had shown previously, but to her surprise he again took her arm, reminding her of the boulders.

'And that lovely dress,' he added. 'Make sure you're keeping it well off the ground; it's exceedingly dusty along here.'

As they reached the end of the avenue a few people strolling in the gardens came into the orbit of light streaming through the Club windows, then were lost again in the engulfing pool of shadows cast by the trees and shrubs and the walls of the building itself. They appeared again, nebulous indistinct figures— people, and yet Liane once again had that feeling that she and Flint were all alone in this dark continent.

As they drew closer to the Clubhouse music drifted out on to the clear night air. Fireflies and beetles hovered among the bushes, and from somewhere among the flowers there drifted a vague indefinable perfume, infusing the air and affecting the senses. For Liane, walking beside the tall silent man whose profile was taut and severe, it was an interlude of confusion of mind. For part of her seemed to be vitally affected by Flint's sudden lack of friendliness, while the other part of her seemed to be straining-at the bonds of consciousness, desiring only to drift languidly into a world of unreality where nothing was tangible enough to give either pleasure or pain.

'Flint—where have you been!' The exclamation, spoken in a deep and husky voice, broke discordantly into Liane's hazy mind and she glanced towards the Club verandah. Alma was sitting at a table, all alone, a cigarette between her scarlet lips. 'I'm feeling dreadfully neglected,' she added as Flint and Liane sat down. 'Where have you been?' she asked again before drawing heavily on her cigarette. Her narrowed eyes were on Liane's face and she seemed to be repressing anger.

'Walking, Alma,' replied Flint pleasantly. 'Liane and I were wanting a breath of fresh air.'

'Well, you might have invited me to join you,' pouted Alma. 'I felt like a breath of fresh air too.'

Flint looked at her, his manner one of detachment.

'You're getting fresh air now—out here.'

'I wanted to walk, though.' Alma paused to light another cigarette; her eyes, dark and beautiful, held a tempting expression when presently she added, 'Come with me now, Flint——' And she turned her head towards Liane and said with a sort of acid sweetness, 'You don't mind, Miss Goulden?'

'Of course not,' replied Liane, and she did wonder, afterwards, if it was the indifference in her voice which made Flint rise at once and say,

'In that case, we'll take that walk, Alma. Liane, please excuse us.'

A moment later it was Liane who was alone on the verandah, her big blue-green eyes following the two tall distinguished figures until they disappeared into the misty darkness of a clump of trees.

# CHAPTER FOUR

For Liane the following two weeks were somewhat hectic. She attended another dance at the Club, and a party given by Jim Berger for his wife's birthday. She visited the beautiful home of the Van der Galts where a superb dinner had been put on for their guests. At all these functions Liane's unique dress sense had brought forth spontaneous and sincere comments, and even when, at the barbecue given by Mark and Kirsty, she wore only casual slacks and a shirt, remarks were still made.

Only one person showed a complete lack of appreciation—Alma. Not once had she commented on what Liane wore. Not that Liane wanted her to; in fact, the assertion by Kirsty that she was now acclaimed as the best-dressed woman in and around Ravensville merely served to make Liane feel extremely embarrassed. True, she enjoyed being well-dressed; she knew her clothes were distinctive and that she wore them with an air of confidence and *savoir vivre*—traits which she had acquired by going about with her boss—but she had no desire to impress anyone other than Richard. This she had failed to do and therefore the praise from others meant nothing at all. Flint, cool now with her and perplexingly sardonic at times, nevertheless showed his appreciation whenever they met.

'Your dress is charming, Liane,' had been his comment when he saw her at the Van der Galts' dinner party.

'Your taste in dress is impeccable,' he had stated on another occasion.

'Another delightful creation!' had brought forth the pettish remark from Alma,

'In design, yes, but white is so insipid, Flint.'

One or two people standing close had stared in surprise at this outright show of bad manners on Alma's part but, strangely, Flint heard it without any sign that it was in bad taste.

'Flint seems to be more interested in Alma than ever,' Kirsty said on the evening of the barbecue. 'I do hope he isn't serious; I'd hate to have her for my nearest neighbour.'

'They are alike in many ways,' mused Liane, her eyes seeking the pair as they stood beneath the trees over by the charcoal stove. 'Both extraordinarily good-looking.'

'I agree about that. But Alma's so hard.'

'So is Flint—according to you,' Liane reminded her cousin in some amusement. 'I think that probably he and Alma would get along tolerably well together.'

'Mark's still of the opinion that Flint isn't really serious about Alma.'

Yet the two were seen together very often, and gossip about them was rife, with people openly declaring that an engagement was certain to be announced in the near future. All invitations extended to one were also extended to the other.

'Flint's aunt'll be arriving tomorrow afternoon.'

64

Kirsty passed on the information to Liane as they sat in the garden of Gimbulu Farm, in the lambent golden glow of early evening. 'I'm dying to see what she's like, because I can't by any stretch of imagination see Flint exhibiting patience with anyone so old.'

'You can't? Why?' Liane, like her cousin, was attired in very brief shorts and a sun-top. Both girls reclined in garden loungers covered with gaily-coloured linen.

'I can't explain why,' returned Kirsty. 'It's just that a very old woman and Flint don't seem to go together.'

'He told me he's giving her a birthday party while she's here.'

'She must be eighty-one, then? I remember Flint once mentioning that he had an eighty-year-old aunt who comes to visit him at regular intervals.'

'Yes, she'll be eighty-one while she's with him.'

'She's a spinster, I believe.'

'That's right.'

Kirsty's eyes widened.

'Flint told you?'

'He mentioned it, yes.'

'He's usually so reserved.' Kirsty spoke thoughtfully, a rather odd inflection in her voice. 'Not with you, though,' she added after a pause.

Liane merely shrugged her shoulders.

'At first he seemed to be friendly,' she said.

'At first?'

'He seems to keep his distance now.'

A slight frown settled on her cousin's forehead.

'Has something happened between you?'

'No, of course not.' Liane gave her a puzzled glance. 'I don't know what you mean, Kirsty?'

65

'If Flint was friendly at first, but he's now keeping his distance, then something must have happened to bring about the change.'

Liane inclined her head in agreement, but went on to say that she had no idea what could have brought about the change in Flint's manner towards her. Looking back, Liane knew the change had begun on the night when she and Flint had strolled in the Club grounds, after she had talked about herself, telling him of her job and her employer. She now realised that Flint had shown far more interest than would have been expected when first she knew him. But it had not been very long before he had begun to put questions to her, questions about her life which she had successfully evaded for the most part. But on the night when he and she had walked in the Club grounds, and then strolled to the lovely little glade of which he had spontaneously made her a gift, he had somehow managed to draw her out and she had confided things which she would normally have kept to herself. She now recalled that he had several times drawn a breath of impatience when she told him that she had never hesitated to cancel her own arrangements if her boss happened to need her assistance at a meeting he was attending, probably in another town, which meant spending the night there, or even several nights.

Continuing to reflect on that evening, Liane now wondered just how she had portrayed her employer. Had she inadvertently put him in a bad light? The idea actually hurt, for to say anything derogatory about the man she loved was totally alien to her desire. She wanted only to praise him, to emphasise his good points —his generosity regarding her salary, his insistence that she should occupy first class accommodation at any hotels in which they might stay, his always treating her as an equal.

'I'll have to go and see how the meal's getting along.' Kirsty's voice broke into Liane's thoughts and she turned her head. 'Sylvester's doing one of his specialities. I don't know what it is, but I can smell it from here—and it smells good!' Rising as she spoke, Kirsty reached for a towelling wrap and draped it over her bronzed shoulders. 'You needn't come in yet,' she added with a smile. 'I'll call you a short while before it's ready to put on the table.'

'I'll be in shortly; the sun's going down, so I shan't get any more tan today.'

Kirsty went off towards the homestead and for a while Liane lay back and gazed up at the lazy blue sky that was already taking on a hint of pearly grey. To the right of where she lay was a trellis over which a profusion of scarlet bougainvillaea cascaded down to form a backcloth to a border of roses and canna lilies, while down at the far end of the garden a hedge of pink hibiscus formed yet another background scene for a dainty herbaceous border whose predominant colours were mauve and white. Beyond this rose the line of kopjes, with the sun heading towards them, the sky in its wake now bejewelled with gold.

The soft purr of a car engine suddenly broke into the silence and Liane turned her head, wondering who could be calling at this time. She recognised the car as soon as it came into view and her eyes never left it until its owner, having brought it to a standstill at the front of the house, eased his long slender body from the driver's seat. He was about to walk towards the front door when some instinct made him turn his head. A smile came to his lips as he saw Liane, and he came forward in her direction. She sat up, conscious of her scanty attire, and of the fact that she had left her wrap several yards away, on a low rustic seat shaded by a breadfruit tree. She and Kirsty had been sitting there earlier, when the sun was at its fiercest.

'Hello!' Flint's smile remained while his grey eyes moved with a sort of lazy good-humour over her whole body. 'You're acquiring a most attractive tan, but watch you don't overdo it.'

'I'm taking it steadily.' She paused, but he did not speak. 'If you want Kirsty she's indoors. Mark's still out in the fields somewhere.'

'I merely came over to bring a book I'd promised to lend Mark.' Another silence; Liane's eyes strayed to her wrap and then Flint did speak, saying on a quizzical note, 'Can I get it for you ... seeing that you're feeling so embarrassed without it?'

She coloured instantly, yet she responded to his humour, not having lost her composure to any great extent.

'Thank you, Flint,' she said with a laugh. And she added as he turned, 'You're right; I do feel embarrassed without it.'

He picked it up but stood where he was. And suddenly the air seemed to be charged with electricity. It was as if each expected the other to do something, and so both were waiting.

'You look charming as you are,' he said at last, breaking a silence that, to Liane, had seemed interminable. 'However, as you appear to want this thing, then here it is.' He handed it to her, watching as she put it on

68

and drew the front edges together. But even then his eyes roamed, to her legs and down to her shapely ankles. 'My aunt arrives tomorrow afternoon,' he said conversationally after another pause. 'Will you come over and meet her?'

Liane was surprised by the invitation, remembering as she did that a coolness had developed in Flint's attitude towards her. However, she accepted the invitation graciously, saying she would be delighted to meet his aunt.

'What's her name?' she asked a moment later, after Flint had confidently asserted that she and his aunt would get along famously together.

'Same as mine, Dawson—Miss, as I told you. But I expect she'll ask you to call her Aunt Miriam; she always does.'

Dressed casually in a flared skirt of denim type material with matching short-sleeved shirt, both embroidered with bright red flowers and green leaves, Liane entered the grounds of Kimara Lodge looking cool and fresh; her step was light, her russet hair attractively blown by the faint breeze drifting in from the mountains. Flint was standing by a flower border, talking to his aunt. Turning, he waited till Liane reached them, then the introductions were made.

'How do you do ...' Liane's voice was somewhat faint, for she had received a little shock of surprise at the old woman's appearance. She supposed she had expected to meet someone a little wrinkled at least, and slightly bent about the shoulders. Instead, she gazed admiringly at a tall straight woman with clear features and a remarkably youthful figure. Her smile was charming, her voice musical and low. On closer examination Liane saw that the skin around her mouth and at the corners of her eyes was a little faded, but her dark grey eyes were very soft and sweet.

'I'm happy to meet you, Liane. Flint's mentioned you at least half a dozen times since I arrived—and I haven't been here very long, as you are probably aware.' While speaking she was making a close examination of Liane's face; then her eyes travelled, taking in the slender figure clothed so attractively, the shapely legs and ankles, the blue leather sandals which matched the outfit. Liane, surprised that Flint should have been speaking about her so much, glanced up into his darkly bronzed face and again asked herself why he should be so interested in her. The coolness adopted after that evening at the Club appeared to have dissolved altogether, replaced by the friendliness she had known before.

At this present moment his face was an unreadable mask; Liane sensed his vexation at his aunt's mentioning that he had been talking about her.

'Shall we go on to the stoep and have a drink?' His finely-toned voice brought a nod from his aunt and the three began walking towards the shady, flower-draped verandah in front of the house.

'You must call me Aunt Miriam,' the old lady was saying to Liane a few minutes later when Flint was away getting the drinks. 'I can't abide people addressing me as Miss Dawson.' The grey eyes twinkled and the pale lips smiled. 'Flint tells me you're on holiday with your cousin and her husband?'

'Yes, that's right.'

'I know Mark, of course—charming young man. But

I haven't yet met his wife. It was a surprise to me when Flint mentioned in his letter that Mark had got married.' Aunt Miriam's eyes twinkled again. 'I expect my nephew's told you that I have no time for marriage?'

Liane laughed, marvelling at the ease with which she was getting along with her. But Flint had said that she would like his aunt, Liane recalled.

'He did mention something of the kind, yes.'

'It's true that it only applies to myself. I consider I'm above slaving for some man who takes it all for granted. It has always been my contention that every creature on this earth has its own life to live, and that self must come first.' Aunt Miriam spread her hands. 'If you can give me one good reason why I should have sacrificed my life for another human being, then I'll admit that I've been wrong all these years.' There was a challenge in her voice, a question in her eyes.

'If you'd fallen in love,' said Liane after a pause, 'then you wouldn't have been able to help yourself. You'd have married, eagerly, with never a thought to the less attractive side of marriage.' Suddenly alert, Liane turned her head. Flint was standing there, an expression on his face which Liane found impossible to read. That he had heard what she had said was plain as, coming forward with a silver tray, he said, his eyes never leaving Liane's face,

'So you do believe in marriage? You gave me to understand you had an aversion to it.'

Liane coloured, aware of Aunt Miriam's inquiring stare.

'I said *I* would never marry. I didn't say I had an aversion to marriage in general.'

71

Aunt Miriam glanced from one to the other, the most curious expression on her face.

'So you two have already had a discussion on marriage? How interesting. Might I be so inquisitive, Liane, as to ask why you so firmly state that you will never marry?'

The colour in Liane's cheeks heightened.

'It's a personal matter,' she replied with a trace of apology. 'I'd rather not talk about it.'

The old lady shrugged as if accepting this, but it was plain that she was still a little baffled by Liane's attitude towards marriage.

Flint placed the tray on the table, handed a glass each to his aunt and Liane, then sat down.

'How long have you been here?' inquired Aunt Miriam conversationally.

'Almost three weeks.' Picking up her glass, Liane took a drink of the delicious lemonade. 'I've another three weeks left.'

'So you'll have had six weeks only? It's a long way to come for so short a time.'

'I have a job,' returned Liane, acutely conscious of Flint's absorbed attention. She had noticed a strange, unfathomable expression come to his face when she said she had three weeks of her holiday left. And suddenly she was wondering if he would have liked her to stay longer. The idea seemed totally unacceptable, and yet she found herself unable to reject it.

'What is your job?' Again the old lady spoke conversationally.

'I work in an office.'

'Interesting?'

'Very. I travel with my boss. We were in Paris a few weeks ago, and before that we were in Austria.'

A movement caught her eye and she turned her head, glimpsing the bright yellow plumage of a bird as it flew into the sun-warmed foliage of a bush honeysuckle.

'Paris is heavenly,' Aunt Miriam was saying. 'I could live there—if I could afford it,' she added with a grimace, taking up her tall crystal tumbler from the table and moving the orange liquid against the light. 'You're a very fortunate young lady to have a job that takes you to such interesting places.'

Liane fell silent, dwelling on the word 'fortunate'. She had always considered herself to be far more privileged than any of the young women of her acquaintance, but not now. She realised that it would have been far better if she had never gone to work for Richard Wilding because then she would never have found herself in such an unhappy situation as she was in at the present time.

'What are you thinking about, Liane?' Soft the tone, but insistent. She looked at Flint across the table; there was a quiet, ironic quality about him which baffled her.

'You asked me something of the kind once before,' she said, managing to inject a lightness into her tone which was emphasised by a brief laugh. 'I told you that one's thoughts are something which one can always keep private.' Her eyes went to Aunt Miriam's face and she saw the puzzlement in the dark grey eyes.

'You brood too much,' he told Liane.

She stared, at this plain manner of speaking, and decided to change the subject, remarking on the beauty of Flint's gardens and gesturing unconsciously in the direction of a pergola, draped with wistaria.

'Flint's fortunate in that all this was planted a long time ago,' commented Aunt Miriam. And then, 'Have you a nice garden at home, Liane?'

'No, I've a flat, high up in a block.'

'You sound as if you live alone?'

'I do. My parents are dead, and I'm an only child.'

The old lady frowned, opened her mouth to ask a question, then closed it again, merely saying,

'You're young, dear, to be on your own. Have you other relatives—aunts, cousins?'

'I had an uncle somewhere up in Cumbria, but I don't know either where he lives or if he's still alive. He was married, but had no children—so my mother told me. He was her brother.'

'It's rather sad the way members of a family who have once been close can drift apart later in life.' Aunt Miriam looked across at her nephew. 'Flint's always kept in touch with me, and I'm grateful——'

'My love——' interrupted Flint, but he himself was immediately prevented from saying anything else.

'I feel I've somewhere to come when I want to be near one of my own. And I know I'm always welcome in this lovely house——'

'Aunt Miriam,' said Flint firmly, 'shall we talk of something more interesting?'

'Never did like flattery,' she told Liane laughingly. 'Proud and stiff at times—and adopts an air of superiority—but you must have noticed, my dear?'

Liane only laughed, catching the old woman's humour and not caring if Flint should happen to be annoyed. He showed no sign of annoyance, however, as he began to explain his relationship to his aunt. Miriam was the daughter of Flint's maternal grandmother by a

74

marriage previous to that which produced Flint's mother.

'So,' interposed Miriam, 'I am really only a half-aunt, so to speak. Hence it has amazed me that he shows such concern. He'd have had me live with him had I wanted to do so, but I prefer my independence until the time comes when it's impossible for me to retain it.'

Flint had raised his straight dark brows and it was plain that he was waiting for his aunt to stop speaking so that he could say what was hovering on his lips.

'It amazes you that I show concern? What kind of a man would I be if I didn't, after what you did for my mother?'

'Oh, that,' carelessly and with a wave of her hand which was made as a dismissal of the subject. 'It was nothing, Flint——'

'Nothing?' Again his eyebrows were raised. He turned to Liane. 'My mother was a widow by the time I was seven years old; a year later she was an invalid. Aunt Miriam, in her fifties by this time, dropped everything that was important to her and came to look after us both——'

'Flint, dear——'

'She stayed on here until my mother's death—when I was almost twenty. And it was only then that she went back to her own home in Pretoria, and resumed the independent life which she spoke of just now.'

Aunt Miriam had coloured a little, but her composure was in no way impaired.

'Flint's always so eloquent and convincing, Liane, but I assure you there was no sacrifice on my part. I lived bed and board free for all those years, drawing a

75

good rent for my own house at the same time. I ended up with a big bank balance which now enables me to enjoy life to the full.'

Flint laughed briefly, his eyes holding a gleam of humour.

'If anyone's eloquent and convincing, Aunt Miriam, it's you! I should have learned, long ago, that in an argument with you I must lose.'

His aunt bypassed this but talked for a little while about those years when she had lived at Kimara Lodge, and now and then Flint would interrupt to add something. Listening intently, Liane gained a fairly comprehensive picture of Flint's early life, of those years before he took over the full responsibility of the vast estate which was his inheritance. In addition to much else Liane learned that Flint owned an extensive forest to the south of Ravensville, and this was looked after by no fewer than twelve boys. The little glade, of which Liane was now the owner, was on the edge of this forest.

At last the subject was exhausted and Liane said she must be leaving.

'It's been a great pleasure for me to meet you,' she said sincerely, turning to Aunt Miriam. 'I hope we shall have another chat before I leave Africa.'

'I'm sure we shall, dear ...' Aunt Miriam's voice trailed away and Liane noticed that the reason for this was something she had seen on her nephew's face. Liane glanced at him, aware that an incomprehensible silence on his part had followed her own words about leaving Africa. Inevitably she recalled his strangeness on a previous occasion when she had mentioned leaving; she remembered having the idea that he would like her to stay longer. Some strange turbulence entered into her and she turned aside on the pretext of finding interest in the flowers growing in ornamental pots on the patio below. Yet Flint's presence was distinctly felt; there was a repelling quality about him, she thought, and when at length she turned again it was to encounter a taut, almost harsh expression on his bronzed and handsome face.

'Something wrong, Flint?' His aunt's voice came as a relief to Liane, for even the air around her seemed filled with an indefinable tension. 'You look positively aggressive!'

His grey eyes came slowly to hers, their expression mask-like.

'I'll accompany Liane back to Gimbulu,' he said, ignoring her comment. 'I shan't be long.'

'I'll come to the end of the garden with you,' she said, rising from her chair. 'The exercise will do me good.'

The three walked abreast for some distance and then Aunt Miriam somehow detached herself from the other two. Liane's attention was arrested by her movements as she went on ahead, a tall graceful woman carrying herself proudly—as proudly as her nephew, decided Liane, an admiring light in her eyes. The dress she wore was fairly long; it fell about her slender body in lines of dignified simplicity. To watch her walk across the lawn was an education in itself, and Liane's admiration grew with every moment that passed. She knew she would experience a deep sense of regret when she said her last goodbye to Aunt Miriam.

# CHAPTER FIVE

SHE was alone beneath the stars, sitting on a smoothed-out ledge in the rocks, feeling totally at peace, and a little proud of the fact that she was the owner of all she surveyed.

'Liane's Glade ...' she murmured into the purple and silver night. 'I wonder why he made me a gift like this?' She glanced around as she spoke, thrilling to the music of running water in her ears as it danced over the rocky slope to enter the star-spangled stream along whose banks flourished a veritable garden of grasses and flowers.

She had come immediately after dinner, which had been served early because Sylvester had asked if he could get away to his native village, as his brother was very ill. The sun had set when Liane arrived at her glade, but night had not come down and for a while she was able to appreciate the colours—of flowers, birds, butterflies and the pretty little lizards which moved so gracefully over the damp rocks. It was a treasure of unplanned, spontaneous beauty, she decided, feeling that nothing of such a small area could surpass it. Trees overhung the stream, their foliage sometimes trailing the water; the pale light of evening had moved across their branches and now starlight was

78

filtering through, shafts of light which contributed to the fairytale-like impression, and the magic of the whole scene. At her feet grew tiny bulbous cups, seed pods of some delightful little flower that had bloomed earlier in the year.

As the sun disappeared so the shadows had floated down to throw a mist over the surrounding landscape and now, as she sat on the little ledge, with only the sound of water in her ears, she looked up and away from her glade, to the drowsy bushveld and the changeless eminence of the mountains beyond. Lazy colours drenched in moonlight filled the intervening space between her glade and the gate beyond which was the long avenue of blue-gums that led eventually into the grounds of the Sunset Club. Liane gave a contented sigh, and wondered why Richard seemed so nebulous and unimportant. It was as if he were a part of her life that had been lived in the far distant past; this was the present ... and reality. Reality ...? A strange word to come to her mind, she mused, for everything about this lovely glade was magical and, therefore, unreal.

'I wonder why he gave it to me?' she said again, and this time she was surprised to hear her voice carry, as if the water had caused it to echo.

Surprise became amazement when she heard an answering voice, and for a few seconds her pulses quickened.

'I'm glad you've asked that question, Liane. Keep on doing so; you might find the answer.'

'Flint! Oh, but you scared me!'

'Sorry. I did try to crack a few twigs underfoot as I drew closer.'

'You knew I was here?' A frown of bewilderment

creased her wide brow as she glanced up, into his incredibly attractive features. She noted what he wore—the white safari jacket, the blue shirt beneath it. He looked superb, was her subconscious declaration as she listened to him say,

'No, I didn't know you were here. I came to the Club to pick up some books which had been left here for me, and I thought I'd wander along to your glade—just for a few minutes. I was almost here when I saw you, a lovely nereid sitting on her rock——' Breaking off, he laughed down into her flushed face. 'I seem always to be causing you embarrassment, don't I, Liane?' Soft the tone ... almost tender in its vibration. Liane, enveloped as she already was with a sense of unreality, was suddenly unable to control her emotions and she became disturbingly stimulated by Flint's unexpected presence. And now, for the first time, she was admitting, most reluctantly, that she was not totally immune to Flint's attractions, that whenever they met she was conscious of something unusual in the atmosphere. She vividly recalled her repeated impressions that he would like her to stay longer in Africa; she remembered her cousin's assertion that love came naturally, and quickly. If it were meant to be that she and Richard should get together he would have fallen in love without any help from her. Well, it had not come to Richard ... but had it come to Flint—naturally and quickly, and without any help from her? Flint in love with her ... Liane shook her head, dismissing the idea as crazy, an illogical fantasy ... and yet ...

She looked at him through her clear blue eyes and said huskily,

'What did you mean, Flint, when you said—just now —that I might find an answer to my question? Please tell me why you gave this beautiful little glade to me?'

Flint made no immediate reply. The shaft of a smile hovered on the finely-chiselled mouth and his eyes held a tinge of uncertainty. It would seem that he wanted to tell her something but was held back for some reason.

'Perhaps the time is not yet, my dear,' he said at last. 'Just do as I say, and keep on asking yourself why I should give this place to you.' His voice was low, with that tender note plainly in evidence. His eyes were on her, a softness in their depths which, decided Liane, would never have fitted in with that 'flint-like' quality described by her cousin.

'I'm very bewildered,' she began, half wishing she had not come here this evening. For she was becoming more and more deeply affected by Flint's presence, aware of the romance of the setting they were in—the high moon which had come up to throw the stars into shade, the scented breeze and the music of the waterfall, the silence and the impression of being alone in the world, just Flint and herself. It was a sensation she had experienced on a previous occasion.

'Bewildered, dear?'

Dear ... Just now it had been *my* dear.

'I don't—don't understand you, Flint.' Where was her confidence? She felt weak and very feminine—and she found this extraordinarily pleasant. 'You—you puzzle me?'

For answer to this half-question Flint stooped from his great height and, taking her hand in his, pulled her unresistingly to her feet. It was a moment of breathless suspense with Liane's every nerve out of control. There

81

was temptation in the air, magic in the isolation, the call of nature in the primordial silence. And suddenly she was helpless, unable to resist as his lips came down to possess her own in a kiss that was as demanding as it was tender. For a few moments she stood passive, and then, with a partial return to sanity, she found all her instincts rebelling as her loyalty to Richard rose within her. She began to struggle ... then stopped, for an intoxicating lightness of body deprived her of all strength to resist as, stimulated by something more forceful than she had ever known, she surrendered totally to the passionate demand of his lips.

No words were spoken for a long moment and then Flint, taking his mouth from hers for a few seconds, murmured softly,

'Liane ... you're so lovely.' His voice, throbbing with tender passion, mingled with the music from the stream to become part of the wonder and magic that was casting its spell upon her. The blood pulsed through her veins; her arms went willingly around Flint's neck and she lifted her lips in a sweet and seductive invitation. Softly he laughed, and took his fill of what was offered, possessive mastery melding with a gentleness which seemed out of place in so passionate a scene. Liane, thrilling to his dominance, found an exquisite, sensual enjoyment in her voluntary surrender. For his part, Flint was triumphant; she sensed this in his increased ardour and, carried on the tide of this ardour, Liane gave herself up entirely to the delights of the moment. Nothing in the whole of her world mattered except this; no inner warning thrust itself into her consciousness to tell her there would be regret later; no intrusion of her employer's rugged face rose to remind her that he was the man she loved. It was as if no other being existed and she was free—free to take and give and in so doing be carried into the very realm of heaven itself.

At last he held her from him, and she supposed it was his words which brought the first thread of sanity.

'Liane—I can't believe it's true, can't believe that you love me.'

'Love!' Her glance was both startled and dismayed. 'Flint—you've——'

'Yes, love,' he interrupted softly, his adoring gaze fixing hers. 'Your kisses are like a heady wine——'

'Flint,' she broke in urgently, full sanity rapidly returning, to bring with it both shame and regret. 'You don't understand.' She stopped, wondering how she could possibly explain her conduct. It was clear that Flint loved her ... and because of her eager reciprocation, he had taken it for granted that his love was returned.

'I do understand, my sweet.' Flint's soft and tender voice came to her before she could find anything to say. 'You love me, and not this man you work for——'

'Richard?' she frowned. 'How do you know about my loving him?' Embarrassment brought the colour flooding into her cheeks and she turned aside.

'You inadvertently betrayed your feelings for him on that day when you were telling me about your life in England, and your job.' Flint paused and gently turned her face round again. She looked into his eyes, saw the expression they held—and she knew that if she had seen that expression in Richard's eyes she would have been deliriously happy. 'On our very first meeting I strongly suspected that you were going to

83

have a vital effect on my life,' Flint was continuing, and although Liane knew an urgent desire to stop him she could not speak for the terrible blockage in her throat, caused both by her own misery and by the knowledge that, for the first time in her life, she was going to subject another human being to pain and humiliation. 'However, when I learned of your feelings for this Richard I decided there was no hope for me, even though the man was now engaged to someone else. Your reason for coming on this holiday was that of escapism and that in itself was a bar to my chances of winning you. But every time your departure from here was mentioned I felt I must speak to you before it was too late, but no opportunity presented itself.' He stopped and a glimmer of amusement entered his eyes. 'I could scarcely say, right out of the blue, that I loved you and wanted you for my wife. However, fate took a hand and my chance came tonight. Darling Liane, will you——?'

'Flint!' The word came swiftly, forced from her parched lips by the urgency of preventing him from asking a question to which she must answer no. 'I—I don't know wh-what to say to you.' He was still holding her arms, but she was scarcely conscious of the fact. His touch no longer excited her; the ecstatic interlude was over. 'This is so—so sudden.' Not very original, but she was again lost for words, her mind having switched to the passionate scene in which she had played so willing a part. Automatically she twisted from Flint's hold, shame and self-disgust enveloping her like a deluge. To have succumbed both to Flint's passion and her own, and without one word of protest leaving her lips! She was no better than a wanton. Her cheeks burned as her thoughts remorselessly brought back every incident. Side by side with this was her awareness of disloyalty to the man she loved. How could she have allowed another man to embrace her, to kiss her with such unrestrained ardour as Flint had done? More and more blood rushed to her cheeks, and her whole body quivered under the weight of her own self-reproach.

'Liane, dear ...' Flint's voice reached her as from a great distance, 'what's wrong?'

She had moved away and she now felt the cooling spray of the waterfall on her face and arms.

'I feel so ashamed,' she managed at last, her eyes appealing and apologetic. 'I wish I'd never come here tonight.' The reason why she had come was that for the whole of the day Richard had been in her thoughts and her little glade seemed to beckon her, a haven of peace where she could relax her mind and body. Mentioning to Mark and Kirsty that she would like to go there, she had then asked for the loan of her cousin's bicycle. Mark had immediately offered her the loan of the runabout, which she had driven several times when she and Kirsty had gone into Ravensville. The runabout was at this moment in a corner of the Sunset Club car park, but evidently it had escaped Flint's notice when he parked his own vehicle.

'Ashamed?' repeated Flint as if he did not understand. 'Ashamed of what?'

She shook her head dumbly. She was almost in tears, thinking how different it would have been were it Richard standing there, in this lovely moonlit glade. But it was not Richard; it was a man she could never love because her heart was already given to her employer. Yet suddenly it was Flint that mattered for he was the one who shortly would be hurt. His sincerity tormented her conscience, and the anxious expression that now lingered in his dark eyes was in itself a potential accusation that pierced everything that was decent in her. What could she do? There was no way but absolute honesty, she admitted and, looking across at him she said, in a voice little above a whisper,

'I don't know what came over me, Flint, but I'm thoroughly ashamed of myself. Never before have I—I lost control——' The words were so difficult; she could not meet his hardening gaze as she added, determined to go on, and not to spare herself in the process, 'The blame is all mine—the blame for what happened just now, I mean; I ought not to have allowed you to kiss me, or to—to say those tender things ...' She tailed off, again experiencing the greatest difficulty in voicing what was in her heart and mind. 'You see, Flint, I still love Richard.' It was out at last, and a terrible silence followed. She turned at length, and gave a little gasp at the harshness displayed on his face. His mouth twisted out of all recognition as he said,

'You don't love me?' Low and rasping his voice, and his eyes were indeed as hard as flint. 'Yet you responded to my kisses and——'

'Yes, I know I did,' she broke in, wishing she could fly from him, into the mothy darkness of the veld. 'I can't think what came over me; I shall never understand why I responded. It must have been this place——' She gestured expressively to embrace the whole fairytale scene: the starlit water cascading over the rocks, the gently-moving fronded foliage of the tree-ferns through which darts of moonlight shot their silver beams on to the tiny pool and the rivulet that danced away from it to join a larger stream that would eventually carry it to the sea. Lichen-covered boughs glistened from the spray that fell upon them; fireflies glowed among the thorny mimosas, and the slender willows growing by the stream. From the mountains a gentle breeze, passing through the low vegetation of the veld, made soft, tenuous music like that produced by a harp. 'It's all so unreal,' she whispered huskily, 'and I—I must have been carried away ...' She found her voice failing her as she noticed the dark colour creeping along the corners of Flint's mouth. 'I'm so—so very sorry ...'

'Sorry!' It was a snarl that left his lips. 'You enjoyed our lovemaking as much as I did, yet you stand there and say you shouldn't have allowed me to kiss you! And then you tell me you're sorry! What sort of a woman are you?' He was incensed with fury and Liane knew this fury had resulted from the deep humiliation which had been inflicted upon him. He was not the kind of man to open up his heart very often. On the contrary, he was of a reserved, aloof disposition, his manner often one of hauteur and cool superiority. There was a nobility about his bearing which matched to perfection the aristocratic features which gave him that handsome yet formidable appearance.

Liane moved uneasily under his smouldering stare, and wished again she could escape.

'I can't blame you if you condemn me for my conduct,' she said huskily at last. 'As I said, I don't know what came over me——' She broke off, shaking her head. 'That's not my normal conduct—please believe me?' She looked appealingly at him; it suddenly seemed important that he should not conclude that she was in the habit of allowing men to kiss her. 'I wish I'd been more controlled——'

'That's enough!' He was tight with anger still, but it was evident that he had no intention of suffering any further indignity, either by a violent show of temper or by prolonging this scene. 'You're embarrassing us both by your self-condemnation.' He looked at her, his hard eyes dark with contempt. 'The sooner we forget what's happened here tonight the better we shall both feel!' And without another word he left her, standing there in the little grove which had been his gift to her ... his gift to the girl he loved.

Tears came, the result of nervous tension as much as with regret for what she had done to Flint. That he would never forgive her went without question. She wondered what the rest of her stay would be like and wished she could cut it short and return to England ... and to the man who did *not* love her.

The situation was all so illogical, she reflected, bitter resentment against fate rising within her. Here was a man who loved her and wanted to marry her, yet *she* was in love with a man who did *not* want her, a man who in all the six years she had worked for him had never even noticed her as a woman. Yet Flint had noticed her as a woman at their very first meeting; it had been love at first sight.

She turned to leave, but changed her mind and sat down on the little ledge again. The glade, vibrant with moonlight, was still a romantic place—an idyllic, dreamlike garden fashioned entirely by the hand of nature. The scent of growing things provided an added, elusive charm, as did the dark vault of the sky above, where a million points of light filtered the fine tracery of cirrus clouds.

It was hers. And yet it was not, for even though she knew that Flint would never take it back, she knew also that, even were she to live permanently in Africa, she would never return once she left it this evening.

A deep sadness filled her as at last she rose and followed the path which Flint had taken a short while previously. His car was not on the park, and she could imagine him driving back to Kimara Lodge with his mind filled with contempt for the way she had behaved. For herself, Liane felt she would remember her shameful conduct for the rest of her life.

It was the evening of Aunt Miriam's birthday party and for the whole of the day Liane had been racking her brain to think up some credible excuse for not attending. At last she resorted to a headache, since she could find nothing else. Kirsty, showing concern in her lovely brown eyes, caused Liane to suffer a pang of conscience and she wished she could tell her cousin the truth. However, this was not possible, and Liane could only try to convince Kirsty that there was no need for anxiety.

'It's probably the heat,' she offered, and was not surprised when Kirsty shook her head and reminded her that the heat had not affected her before.

'And you've been here for almost a month,' she added, frowning as she spoke, and Liane guessed that Kirsty was thinking that there were two weeks only left before Liane's holiday came to an end. 'I don't feel like going without you,' she added. 'It doesn't seem right that I should.'

'You're not missing the fun just because of me, Kirsty. I'll be all right; I shall go to bed and rest.' She felt a hypocrite since, physically, she had never been better in her life, the rest and sunshine having done her the world of good. Mentally she was not in such good shape; she brooded often, more over what she had done to Flint than on her own unhappy situation. In fact, she would often find herself receiving a little shock when Richard's image was erased by that of Flint.

'You're sure?' Kirsty was still anxious. 'I'll willingly stay with you.'

'It isn't necessary,' Liane assured her earnestly. 'I'd hate it if you insisted on staying at home.'

Kirsty and Mark left a short while later and Liane sat on the stoep, watching the brilliant colours of sunset flare across the arc of the sky. It was a spectacle of which she would never tire, she thought, no matter how long she were to remain in Africa.

Two weeks from now, though, she would be witnessing this miracle for the last time, for in the morning she would be leaving. It was strange, but she had no enthusiasm for her job, for a return to the office where Richard would greet her with his slow smile, inquire if she had enjoyed her holiday, and then plunge her into a round of activity, every aspect of which would be urgent. Do this, Liane; see to that. Make an appointment with Walker and Brown, and another with Thomsons. Oh, yes, I forgot—we shall be going up to Manchester cn Friday so don't come to work without your toothbrush. And so it would go on, with Richard relying on her, as usual. Yet he had managed without her for a month, and he would continue to do so for another fortnight. Faintly Liane smiled. Once and once only had she been off work with an illness; on her return everything was in chaos. She wondered if it would be the same again. This possibility brought a frown to her forehead. She felt she could not face a time so hectic as that had been.

The sun was sinking rapidly and the dappled shades of twilight began to vanquish the gold and flame and crimson. The kopjes became indistinct shapes rising above the drowsy bushveld, while above them stars began to garland the sky. There was the promise of a magical African night, with the immense and timeless landscape slumbering beneath the mystic radiance of the moon.

Liane had just decided to go into the house when the sound of a car caught her ears and she looked towards the road. Headlights flared; the next moment the vehicle had entered the drive of Gimbulu Farm and her heart turned a somersault as she recognised the car.

Flint ... What could he want? He knew she was alone, since Kirsty and Mark were over at his house. She and he had met only once since that incident in the glade; Flint's attitude towards her had been one of near indifference, although he had had to be cautious because Kirsty and Mark were present too.

The crunching of the car coming to a standstill caused something to vibrate in her veins and she rose from her chair with the intention of dodging into the house before he caught sight of her. She was too late; Flint was already striding towards the stoep. In a sort of self-defensive gesture she reached up and snapped on the light. Taking the steps two at a time, Flint stopped, his hard grey eyes meeting hers in a look of disdain. She swallowed, standing stiffly erect, and waited for him to speak.

'Kirsty said you were going to bed.'

Puzzled, Liane nodded and again waited for him to speak.

'You're supposed to have a headache.'

'Yes—yes, I have——'

'You blush when you lie. Have you a headache?' he asked, and Liane could only produce a stumbling negative. 'My aunt expected to see you at her party; she was bitterly disappointed when you failed to arrive.' Flint's voice was cold, impersonal, but his grey eyes bored into her. She felt the strength of his contempt while at the same time being aware that he was about to ask her to come to the party. In an attempt to forestall him she said,

'I can't come to your house, Flint. I'm sorry. Please convey my sincere apologies to your aunt. I've sent a small present with Kirsty——' She stopped as the muscles round his mouth contracted. It was plain that his aunt's happiness on this occasion of her birthday was of the utmost importance to him.

'Why can't you come?' he demanded almost harshly.

'How can I be a guest in your home after—after——?'

'There's no need to bring *that* up,' he cut in harshly. 'I told you to forget it!' He paused a moment. 'Are you coming to Aunt Miriam's party?'

Automatically she shook her head, saw his eyes darken beneath their hooded lids, giving him a formidable expression.

'I should feel uncomfortable,' she confessed. 'After what happened——'

'I've told you to forget it!'

'I'm sorry. It's difficult for me to forget, because I feel so blameworthy.'

Ignoring this, Flint asked her again if she was coming to the party, adding in cool, brusque accents,

'As I've said, my aunt was bitterly disappointed when you didn't arrive. She seems to have taken an extraordinarily strong liking to you, and to be quite honest I don't think any of the other guests matter much to her at all.'

A trifle dazed by this, Liane puckered her forehead in a frown and murmured,

'I can't think why. I've met her only twice.' Yet she recalled how she herself had taken to Aunt Miriam and knew she would experience regret on saying goodbye for the last time.

'She's always been rather eccentric in some things,' was his comment, which was not very flattering to Liane. 'There are occasions when it's impossible to account for how she thinks, and acts.' Liane said nothing. She was fully sensible of the fact that although Flint wanted her to go to the party, he could never bring himself to plead with her. She looked at him, immaculate in an off-white suit of linen, his bronzed features cold and forbidding even though his eyes held anxiety in their depths. He was a wonderful person, really, she thought, wanting as he did for this evening to be one that his old aunt would remember as a happy time. What right had she, Liane, to spoil everything for her?

'I'll come,' she said with decision. 'I'll have to change, though.'

She almost heard the indrawing of his breath which

betrayed his relief that she had agreed to attend the party.

'Of course. I'll wait here.'

'I'll be as quick as I can.'

It was a quarter of an hour later that she returned, having dressed hurriedly, and yet in spite of this she was quite happy with her appearance. She wore a long evening gown with a halter neck. Of a colour rather lighter than slate blue, it fitted tightly at the waist, flowed down in gathers to what should have been the hemline. But then the material folded over, came up to drape her shoulders, and fastened with a diamanté clip at the front. In effect, the garment was a dress and evening cloak all in one, the skirt of the dress dividing into two parts by being split from about nine inches above the ankle, thus giving the two sides to the cloak. A half-inch trimming of silver lamé, starting at a point where the skirt divided, followed the two edges of the cloak right up to the neckline.

Flint's interest when she appeared was unmistakable. He was unable to take his eyes off her and his stare lasted for what seemed an eternity before he said, obviously forgetting for the moment all that had recently passed between them,

'You look enchanting, Liane.'

She blushed, embarrassment sweeping over her because she, unlike Flint, was thinking of that intimate scene and feeling thoroughly ashamed of herself. Flint's flattery only added to her discomfiture and she would rather he had refrained from passing any comment at all. However, it seemed that he was fascinated by the dress and, looking at the point where it touched the floor, he commented in a puzzled voice,

'The dress and cloak won't separate—or have I, as a mere male, missed something?'

She had to smile.

'No, you haven't missed anything. There's only one garment really.'

'Turn around.' The tone was edged with command and something quickened in her veins ... something profoundly pleasant. Obediently she swung round so that her back was to him. She knew that the folds of the cloak, falling elegantly from her shoulders, had something of a Grecian character about them, and she was not in any way surprised when she heard him say, 'The effect is most dramatic. This gown must surely be a Paris model?'

Still smiling, she faced him again.

'It was made in England. Our dress designers are far more gifted than people realise.' Her voice was cool but friendly; her embarrassment had dissolved completely. Flint certainly had a way of acting as if that interlude had never taken place.

'Shall we go?' he was asking after having taken yet another good look at her gown. 'You're going to stop the show!' he added, and this time there was the merest trace of mockery in his voice.

'I don't know what to say to Kirsty.' Liane voiced the thought as it came to her. They were travelling the short distance between his home and Gimbulu Farm and had just passed a squat, iron-roofed bungalow with a weather-worn stone stoep. The gardens were in darkness, but Liane knew that flowers abounded in that garden, and that on three sides it was enclosed by a grenadilla hedge. Liane had thought, on first seeing the tiny homestead with its delightful setting, that something similar would suit her if at any time in the future she should decide to take Kirsty's advice and come out here to live.

'About coming to the party, after all?' Flint glanced sideways at his companion as he spoke. 'She knows I was coming out to Gimbulu to try to persuade you to change your mind. You see, my aunt was very dejected and Kirsty noticed this at once. Aunt Miriam made no secret of her disappointment at your absence. I offered to come to see you, and Kirsty herself suggested that your headache might have gone just as quickly as it came.' No mistaking the sardonic edge to his voice as he spoke about the headache having come quickly. 'We shall have to put on an act,' he continued after a pause. 'I'll ask you to adopt a friendly attitude towards me when Aunt Miriam's anywhere close.'

'I wouldn't think of not acting in a friendly way,' she returned, a trace of meek apology in her tone. 'My conduct was such that I feel obligated——'

'For heaven's sake, Liane,' he broke in wrathfully, 'stop referring to that night! We both regret it, so put it right out of your mind—as I have!'

# CHAPTER SIX

IT was a very gay and fashionable crowd Liane met on entering Flint's large, elegantly-furnished drawing-room. There were the Van der Galts, all fashionably dressed with the two women wearing rather spectacular pieces of jewellery. The Bergers were present, and several of their relatives—people Liane had met at the Sunset Club. Sam and Maisie Viljoens were there, and of course Flint's friend, Alma.

'Oh, you've come, dear!' There was no mistaking Aunt Miriam's pleasure as, her eyes lighting on Liane, she hurried forward, leaving those to whom she was speaking, and extending both her hands towards Liane. 'How is your headache? I do hope it's better?'

Conscious of the sardonic twist of Flint's mouth as he stood beside her, Liane felt the colour rise in her cheeks.

'It's better,' she replied briefly.

'I'm so glad. I felt rather guilty after Flint had left,' she was confiding after she had taken a long admiring look at Liane's dress. 'You see, I feared he might coerce you into coming—just because he knew how deep my disappointment was. He didn't coerce you, did he?'

Liane shook her head.

'No, of course not.'

'Liane——' Maisie Viljoens had come up and was admiring the unusual dress. 'Can I congratulate you on that beautiful gown?—but tell me, what happens when you want to take the cloak off?'

Liane laughed.

'I have to hold it over my arm,' she admitted. 'And when I sit at the dinner table I have to drape it over the back of the chair.'

'Well ...' It was Aunt Miriam who murmured the one short word.

'I think it's quite exceptional,' from Marthe Van der Galt with interest. 'Do you suppose my dressmaker in Ravensville could copy it for me? And would you mind if she did?'

'No, I wouldn't mind at all.' The answer came spontaneously and with a smile. 'If she wants to borrow it she can do.'

'I shall of course choose an entirely different colour,' promised Marthe. 'Although I do think that colour is most distinctive.'

'It doesn't make any difference to me if you choose this colour,' returned Liane. 'There'll be no fear of our clashing anywhere because I shan't be here.' It was inevitable that she should glance up at Flint as she said this. His face was an inscrutable mask. He met her eyes and said,

'I'll get you a drink. What would you like?' She told him and he moved away. It was Kamau who brought her the drink on a tray, and Liane was sipping it when Alma came up to her. There was a smooth sort of satisfaction in her voice as she said, after waiting for a

98

moment until Aunt Miriam and Marthe began to converse together,

'I believe you'll be leaving here quite soon now?'

'In about a fortnight's time. I came for only six weeks—but I thought everyone knew that.'

Alma's eyes were travelling over Liane's figure, taking in the classical yet seductive lines of the dress.

'Did I hear you saying that you can't separate that cloak from the dress?'

Liane nodded her head. She had no desire to be unfriendly with the girl, but there was so much undisguised animosity in Alma's attitude towards her that Liane desired nothing more than to get away and mingle with some of the other guests.

'It seems rather silly to me,' commented Alma, her concentration still on the dress, 'that you can't take off the cloak and leave it in a powder-room or somewhere. For myself, I'd find it most tiresome to know that I had to carry the cloak around with me all the while.'

'It's no trouble. In any case, I only take it off when I'm dining.'

Alma shrugged elaborately.

'Every woman to her own taste in dress. For myself —well, I wouldn't dream of wearing the type of clothes which you favour.'

Liane gasped at the sheer rudeness of the girl. But she refrained from answering and instead turned towards the two older women who were conversing at her side. Alma glided away to join Flint; Liane saw her put her arm through his, then look up into his handsome face, making play with her lovely dark eyelashes. There was a profound moment when Flint's eyes flashed to where he had left Liane, and she felt a strange tingling of an emotion as fleeting as it was puzzling. Yet it brought back the memory of her admission, as she stood in her glade, that she was not totally immune to Flint's attractions as a man. He was so different from all other men she had known, so exceptional both in character and looks. Liane supposed that most women would be affected by him, and she recalled Kirsty's saying that all the women who frequented the Sunset Club were crazy about him. Well, mused Liane as she watched Alma with him now, he might marry the girl, and this would put an end to the hopes of all the others.

'Liane dear, I want to thank you for this charming present.' Aunt Miriam's gentle voice dissolved Liane's musings and brought a ready smile to her lips. Marthe had moved away and Liane immediately guessed that Flint's aunt had told her that she wanted to speak with Liane alone. 'It's an antique brooch and I want to know where you managed to pick it up—here, in this out-of-the-way place.' She was wearing the brooch, fingering it almost with affection.

'I already had it,' Liane confessed. 'I knew you'd like it because I saw you wearing something similar—though yours was in gold. This one's silver.'

'And very beautiful. But, Liane, if it was your own——'

'I'm very happy to give it to you,' she said sincerely.

'Then thank you again. I shall be very happy to wear it.' There was a slight pause and then, 'I want to talk to you, my child. We shall go into the garden and have ten minutes together before dinner.'

Although puzzled, Liane agreed to accompany the old lady into the grounds. They were illuminated by lamps hanging from the trees—mangoes and tamarisks, and many other splendid specimens which had matured over a great number of years. Kamau approached them as they reached the french window and were about to step through. Unsmilingly he asked if they wanted drinks.

'No, thank you,' returned Aunt Miriam graciously. 'Not for me.'

'You, miss?'

Liane shook her head.

'No, thank you.' She offered a smile and to her surprise he responded, his white teeth contrasting dramatically with his ebony skin.

'You've scored a victory and no mistake,' declared Aunt Miriam. 'Everyone tries to entice a smile from Kamau, but they all fail. I've been trying for as long as I can remember.' There was a strange ring of satisfaction in her voice, noticed Liane, and she was even more puzzled when she heard the added comment, 'It's almost like an omen.'

'An omen?'

'Take no notice of me, child. I talk to myself quite a lot—you do when you get older, especially if you live alone.'

Liane said, matching her pace to that set by her companion as they made for the path dividing the lawn from the shrubbery,

'Will you ever think of returning to Kimara Lodge? It's obvious that Flint would be happy to have you living with him.'

'What Flint needs is a wife, not an old woman like me.' Liane made no response and after a rather uncertain pause the old lady added, 'Have you noticed how that ridiculous girl Alma toadies to him?'

'I—er——' Liane did not know what to say and suddenly her companion laughed.

'Don't be afraid of speaking your mind, Liane. I hate the creature, as you've instantly guessed. I can't for the life of me see what Flint finds in her. Do you suppose he's using her as a convenience?'

Liane coloured and again the old lady laughed.

'I shouldn't have said that, especially as I've something very important to say to you. Come, we'll sit for a few minutes in my nephew's private little house.'

'Oh—will he not mind?' Liane was recalling how he had said that he came here to be alone; she had sensed that he would resent anyone else entering without his permission.

'He won't know.'

They entered the small grove of mango trees, and then the summer-house, the door of which was unlocked. Aunt Miriam lighted a butane lamp and Liane, becoming more and more mystified with every moment that passed, sat down and waited for the old lady to speak.

'Tell me, Liane,' she said as she herself sat down, 'what's happened between you and Flint?'

Totally taken aback, Liane could only utter a rather flustered,

'I don't know what you mean?'

The old lady looked at her a trifle censoriously.

'I think you do, dear. What made you decide not to come to my party this evening?'

Liane looked down at her hands, wondering what answer she could give that would sound credible, since it was obvious that her excuse of having a headache had been received with no more acceptance than it had with her nephew.

'I don't know what to say.' She looked up uneasily. 'You don't believe I had a headache.' It was a statement, naturally, and Aunt Miriam shook her head.

'Nor did Flint,' she said unnecessarily. 'Liane, my dear, Flint is not very happy these days.' Significant the tone; Liane could find nothing to say. 'When I arrived this time,' continued Aunt Miriam, 'I noticed a marked difference in my nephew. He no longer seemed cynical about love and marriage—— He always had been previously whenever I suggested he look for a wife. He would then remind me of my own attitude towards marriage and tell me he was quite contented with his well-organised existence and he had no intention of allowing a woman to upset it. But this time he seemed to have mellowed, somehow, and I immediately began to wonder if he'd met someone——'

'Aunt Miriam, please don't go on.' Liane spoke urgently, unconscious of her mode of address. It was the first time she had called her Aunt Miriam and the fact that the old lady was pleased escaped her entirely. 'I think we ought to be getting back; dinner will be served any time now.' She half rose, but with an imperative gesture the old lady indicated she should remain where she was.

'The other day Flint inadvertently let it out that he had given you that delightful glade which was part of his forest lands. Now'—there was a second's interruption as Aunt Miriam wagged a forefinger at her—'did you not ask yourself why he should have made you a gift like that?'

'I considered it strange, I suppose, but——'

103

'*Considered?* Surely you attached some importance to it? Flint would hardly be making you a gift that you couldn't enjoy.'

'I did later begin to realise that he—he ...' Liane had too much difficulty in voicing what was in her mind, and she allowed her words to fade away to silence.

'Am I right in thinking that my nephew declared his love for you ... and was told it wasn't reciprocated?'

The forthrightness of the question put Liane out of countenance altogether, and she rose again, this time with more determination than before.

'I'd rather not talk about it,' she murmured. 'Please let's go back to the house.'

'You have answered my question, Liane.' A sadness edged Aunt Miriam's voice as she too rose from her seat. 'You're the first girl he's fallen in love with and you can't love him. It's tragic!' Liane said nothing, but merely stood and watched as Aunt Miriam extinguished the light. At first it seemed that an inky blackness enveloped everything and automatically Liane moved closer and felt for the old lady's hand. 'Thank you, my dear.' Aunt Miriam gave a small sigh and added, 'I took to you in a way I'd never have believed possible, Liane. And when it dawned on me that you were the girl on whom Flint's interest had settled, I was delighted. Most women would be flattered indeed if a man like Flint wanted to marry them,' she went on after a pause.

'Yes—I suppose so,' agreed Liane unhappily. She hated the thought of Aunt Miriam being dejected on her birthday, when Flint had wanted it to be so enjoyable for her. 'He might one day find someone else.'

'If you're thinking of that dreadful Alma—then please don't! Heaven forbid that he'll ever be fool enough to marry her—although there's no knowing what might happen on the rebound.'

'I shouldn't imagine Flint would be so weak as to marry on the rebound, Aunt Miriam.' They had reached the illuminated part of the grounds and Liane took her hand from that of her companion. 'Such an improvident action would be beneath a man of his stature.'

'His pride's been injured,' murmured the old lady almost to herself. 'Yes, his pride's galled because he's lost you.'

'Please don't talk about it,' begged Liane in distress. 'I feel guilty enough as it is.'

'Guilty?' The word was seized upon by Aunt Miriam. 'Is there some reason why you should be feeling guilty?'

'Yes, there is—but I can't talk about it——'

'You gave him encouragement?'

'I didn't discourage him—not soon enough.'

That was all she was intending to say on the matter and with the risk of injuring her own relationship with that of Flint's aunt, Liane abruptly changed the subject and from then on the conversation was light, although a little strained, and it was a relief to Liane when eventually they reached the front of the homestead.

Several people were on the terrace, and one or two others on the stoep, indulging in local gossip, or laughing at a joke which someone had just made. Flint was to be seen in the hall, with Alma close by, one hand gently touching her hair, and in the other a long cigar-

105

ette holder. The fingers of both hands were adorned with rings—an enormous diamond solitaire, a ruby and two emeralds, one encircled with diamonds and the other with tiny pearls. The girl had been left a fortune by a doting uncle, Kirsty had informed Liane, but she had been wealthy before this, having previously inherited a vast amount of property from her grandmother.

As Liane and her companion drew close to the door Liane thought how inviting the aspect was. The ceiling of the porch was illuminated by a rose-coloured lamp, the glow from which fell on the pruned vines curling round the supporting columns, and this reflected radiance was seen also on the white marble steps and the huge urns from which tumbled a riot of flowers and green tracery. All the windows were aglow along the front of the sprawling white homestead, giving the impression of spaciousness and warmth. The light chatter mingled with soft musical strains which Liane surmised came from a tape-recorder somewhere at the back of the large, high-ceilinged hall.

Flint's eyes found hers as she entered with his aunt; Liane saw the narrowing of Alma's gaze as she looked from her to the dignified lady by her side. It almost seemed that the red lips twisted in a sneer and Liane sensed at once that Alma had little or no time for old people.

'Have you been walking?' Flint came over and spoke to his aunt. 'You should have had a wrap, my love.'

'My blood might be a bit thin, but it's not so thin that I'd feel cold on an evening like this. Of course it can get cold later on.'

'It's certainly warm now,' Liane remarked as he

turned to her with an interrogating glance. 'There isn't even a breeze, although there was a light one when we first went out.'

The grey eyes seemed to be lazily indifferent beneath their hooded lids as Flint listened to this, and Liane wondered why he should have bothered to send her that questioning glance. Perhaps, she thought as the idea occurred to her, he was regretting having made the silent inquiry that brought her into the conversation.

Dinner was served shortly afterwards, and then coffee was taken on the stoep and on the terrace. Couples strolled in the brightly-lit grounds of the Lodge, and Liane, having missed Kirsty and Mark, found herself alone by a little sheltered arbour, which she entered and sat for a while, savouring the peace and wondering why she should be thinking of Flint and not Richard. Flint and Alma ... They had been together regularly during the past few days, it seemed. Kathy Van der Galt had mentioned that she had seen them in a café in Ravensville the previous afternoon; Jim Berger had passed the remark, in Liane's hearing, just before dinner, that he expected 'something to be happening' because Flint had been to Alma's home two evenings running.

The sound of footsteps drawing near caused Liane's nerves to tingle but, glancing up as they stopped, she saw Carl standing in front of the arbour with his back to her. He was evidently admiring the flowers and she kept silent, hoping he would move on. Alas for her hopes. He turned and saw her sitting there and a smile lit his face.

'Liane, may I join you in this delightful little spot?'

107

'Of course.' She could hardly say anything else, although she had no desire at all for company. However, she smiled graciously and slid along the seat so that he could take the place beside her. 'It's cool and peaceful here,' she said.

'You wanted to be alone?' he asked, looking uncertainly at her.

'No, of course not,' she lied.

'I've been wanting to tell you how charming you look,' he said. 'You've made all the élite females of Ravensville green with envy.'

She only laughed and passed on to something else, casually remarking on the gardens and the expert planning that had gone into their creation.

'This has been a fabulous party, hasn't it?' he said, bypassing her comments.

'Marvellous. But Flint always does give rather special parties. Kirsty told me this even before I'd been to one myself.'

'There's his *braaivleis* to come yet.'

'It's like our barbecues at home, I think?'

'That's right. We all eat outside. It can be great fun.'

'I'm looking forward to it.' These were the words he would expect to hear, she thought. But at the same time she found herself admitting that she really was looking forward to the *braaivleis*.

'Everything will be on a lavish scale,' said Carl. 'We South Africans always put everything we have into our social events.'

Liane's thoughts went to Richard. She recalled the splendid dinners she had shared with him when they were away from the office on business. Shy and unsure of herself at first, she had gradually become quite used to staying at hotels like the London Hilton and the Savoy. Richard, she knew, was always proud of her and this was evident in the way he so readily introduced her to his business associates. In fact, she had become part of the vast organisation of which he was the head, conversant with every aspect of the complicated manipulations that governed his business empire. Without stint he had praised her ability; without hesitation he had often told his business friends that she was invaluable and that he could not visualise being without her.

And yet, through all this, he had never even noticed her feminine attractions, had never once looked at her in the way Flint had looked at her on that unforgettable evening when he had come to her in her glade.

'Would you care for a stroll, Liane?' Carl's voice broke into her reflections and she turned her head.

'Yes, that would be nice.' She was being polite but cool, for she guessed that Carl was ready to become rather more than friendly.

They walked across the lawn towards the fountain and the pool. Flint was there, silhouetted against the subtly-illuminated backcloth of trees and trellised vines. He looked lonely, she thought, and even as she watched he moved and made his way towards the little clump of mango trees. He wanted to be on his own.

Liane swallowed something in her throat, a feeling of guilt sweeping over her. She could have had him for her husband—a man who loved her dearly. Had she been a hard-headed, practical kind of person, she would have deliberated on the advantages of marriage with Flint, not forgetting the maxim that love begets love. Could she eventually have learned to love Flint? She shook her head, telling herself that she was the kind of girl who could love only once in a lifetime.

'Ah, Liane my dear.' Another voice interrupted her reflections this time, that of Aunt Miriam. 'Have you seen Flint anywhere?'

'He's just gone towards his summer-house,' answered Liane with a smile.

'I see ...' A thoughtful few seconds ensued before the old lady said, 'I wonder if you would go and tell him I want to talk to him?'

'Of course.' The words were out before Liane had time to think that there was no reason why Aunt Miriam should not go to the summer-house and speak to her nephew there.

'Carl will stay with me—to keep me company, won't you, young man?'

'Certainly, Miss Dawson,' he replied with as little hesitation as Liane had shown.

'We'll stroll towards the house. Liane, please tell Flint that there's no urgency. I shall be in the living-room.'

Liane did not try to pretend that the old lady had not engineered this, so that she, Liane, and Flint would be together for a few minutes, in the darkness and seclusion of the copse. What did Aunt Miriam hope to gain? Liane shrugged and went on, carefully holding up her dress so that there was no fear of its touching the ground.

Flint was standing by the open door of the summer-house and he turned his head as she approached from the path at one side.

'Liane—is something wrong?' He was obviously anxious in case something had happened to his aunt and Liane immediately reassured him.

'Your aunt's quite all right, but she wants to speak to you about something. She asked me to come over here and give you the message.'

'How did she know I was here?' Flint's voice was edged with puzzlement and Liane wondered if he was making a guess at his aunt's objective in sending her here, to this lonely and intimate place.

'I told her. I saw you coming towards the mangoes and surmised you were making for the summer-house. Your aunt was looking for you and asked me if I'd seen you anywhere. She said it was nothing urgent,' Liane thought to add.

'I see ...' Even in the dimness Liane could discern the lowering of those hooded lids. 'There appears to be no reason why she couldn't have come here herself,' he murmured, his hard eyes settling on Liane's face. She felt uncomfortable, fully aware now that Flint was as perceptive as she regarding the reason for his aunt's having sent her here.

'I'll be going, then,' she managed presently. 'Your aunt will be in the living-room.' Suddenly she shivered, and automatically drew her cloak more closely around her.

'Are you cold?' asked Flint, and despite the coolness of his tone there was no mistaking the tinge of anxiety in it.

'Someone walked over my grave,' she laughed. 'I'm all right now.'

'That cloak's not very serviceable,' he frowned. 'You should have learned by now that our nights can be very cold.'

Liane knew this. Mark had explained that often there would be frost on the mealie stalks in July, the drop in temperature resulting from radiation into a clear, cloudless sky. However, it was not really cold at present, although Liane was again feeling rather chilly.

'Shall I tell your aunt that you're on your way?' she asked, turning to go.

'You said it wasn't urgent?'

'That's right.' Liane was becoming more uncomfortable with every moment that passed. She wondered if she were imagining it, or whether Flint really was anxious for her to remain with him for a while.

'Then I'll not be back for a few minutes.' He paused, as if waiting to see if she would leave him. Awkwardly she moved from one foot to the other, while her brain was busy trying to find something to say. 'You have no need to stay any longer,' he said at last in a tone of harsh dismissal. 'Tell my aunt I'll be with her shortly.'

'Yes.' Liane moved away, feeling she had been snubbed and discovering to her amazement that the snub hurt abominably.

Nor did she feel any better as she proceeded through the mango trees towards the lights and the laughter drifting over the gardens from the direction of the open windows of the homestead. What was the matter with her? She felt restless, but it had nothing to do with Richard. She realised all at once that she could have stayed for a while with Flint ... that she had *wanted* to stay with him!

What was the matter with her? she asked herself again. There was a hollowness within her which she attempted to ignore, but without success. It seemed to be inextricably linked with her admission that she was not totally immune to Flint's attractions. His face rose before her, obliterating every other image. His charm,

112

his impeccable manners, his air of good breeding, the way he wore his clothes, his strong, finely-timbred voice, his distinctive walk, as if his lithe body was on air ... All these attributes crowded in on her mind so that no room existed for any other pictures to intrude ... not even the past, and the future. Nothing but the present—this lovely garden with the gentle hills beyond and the slumbering bushveld sweeping towards them.

The gay throng of people, Flint's friends; and his aunt, that charming lady of quality who had taken an immediate liking to Liane.

And there was Flint ... the tall bronzed Afrikaner whose wife she could have been.

'Ah, there you are!' Carl's voice was like a rasp as it cut into her reverie and she had difficulty in holding back the frown that came to her brow. 'Flint's aunt didn't want my company after all, so I waited here for your return.'

'That—that was nice of you,' she rejoined with a forced smile. 'I think we should go inside, though. I felt the cold just now.'

'Oh ...' Disappointment tinged his voice. 'If that's what you want?'

She nodded her head.

'In any case, it's getting late. I expect Mark will be wanting to leave soon.'

They entered the house and Kirsty immediately came up to them.

'Isn't it a fabulous party!' she exclaimed in her usual exuberant manner, and with her light brown eyes all aglow. 'Mark wants to go, but I'm not ready yet.'

'Then we'll stay,' from Mark as he came up to them,

his good-humoured face wreathed in smiles as he looked at his wife. 'Another hour won't make any difference.'

'Isn't my husband the most accommodating man in the world!' Lovingly Kirsty tucked her arm in his, and it was at that moment that Flint made his appearance. A sardonic expression entered his eyes as he looked for a moment at Kirsty and Mark, standing so close together, and so very much in love that they didn't care if everyone knew. Flint's eyes wandered to Liane, and then to the man at her side.

And suddenly Liane wished Carl were not with her, that his hand had not crept around her waist, that he was not looking at her with such undisguised admiration. She felt the colour rise to tint her cheeks; she saw the curl of Flint's mouth which seemed to indicate contempt. The next moment she was looking at his broad back as he walked away towards the room in which he would find his aunt awaiting him.

# CHAPTER SEVEN

THE sun was low and the shadows lengthening when Liane returned from her ramble along the bank of the river. She had set out immediately after lunch, overcome by a yearning to be alone. Kirsty was going into Ravensville, as she had an appointment with her dressmaker. She invited Liane to come along, but warned her that the hours might pass with tedious slowness, for the dressmaker not only took a great deal of time with the fitting, but she also chattered so much before and afterwards that the whole of the afternoon would most likely be taken up. Liane politely declined the offer and Kirsty with a grimace said she did not blame her.

'What will you do, though?' she had inquired, her big brown eyes anxiously searching Liane's face. 'I suspect, love, that you've been brooding again, and I don't want you to sit alone for the whole of the afternoon, thinking of that Richard.'

Managing a smile Liane assured her cousin that there was no likelihood of this.

'He seems to be fading from my mind,' she confessed, then added, 'I expect it's this dramatic change in my surroundings. There are so many other things to occupy my time.'

'Well, I'm glad about that, Liane. But what about when you return to the office?'

'It'll all come back,' Liane had to admit, and a terrible feeling of dejection swept down on her momentarily.

'If you had any sense at all you'd throw up that job and settle here——'

'It's impossible, Kirsty. You don't understand just how much Richard relies on me.'

Kirsty frowned darkly but, with admirable restraint, held back the words she would dearly have liked to utter.

'I'll have to be off,' she was saying a moment later, as she glanced at her watch. 'What will you do with yourself?' she asked again, and it was then that Liane, desiring to get right away, even from the servants and the sound of African boys singing in the fields, said she would go for a long walk.

'Don't get lost,' warned Kirsty as she tripped away towards the place where her husband had left the station wagon, all ready for her, facing the gate.

'I won't.'

'See you some time!'

Liane watched until the vehicle had disappeared from sight in a cloud of umber-coloured dust, and then she had turned towards the distant line of trees which denoted the bed of the river.

The ramble had been arduous for the most part, owing to the fierceness of the sun's rays shining down from a clear azure sky. She had come upon small, delightful scenes which had caused her to tarry in appreciation. There were the little wild places, haunts of birds and strange plants; there were small copses where the ground, dark and damp, was strewn with mosses, while climbers sought for the light by reaching for the tops of the trees. Along the river bank glamorous colours were made even more spectacular by the gold of the sunrays as they filtered the foliage of willows; long grasses, rippled by the breeze, turned from green to silver-grey. Sometimes, wonders were disclosed in rapid succession, as when she had come upon a slope sprinkled with brilliant violet flowers which seemed to be attracting several species of bright-winged insects whose colours shone, iridescent in the sunshine; and then, as she turned, a glow of yellow met her eyes, created by a huge clump of gladioli growing on a little abandoned meander some distance from the stream itself. Peach-coloured orchids vied in beauty with their tawny-striped cousins, while in another direction was seen—against the clear sky—the delicate fragile branches of a thorn tree, its foliage creating a lacy cover for two gaily-plumaged birds that glided into it.

During the first hour or so Liane had managed to enjoy the mental relaxation for which she had craved on first setting out from England on this holiday. She had known complete freedom from anxiety about the future. The wonders of nature had acted like a balm, or a drug, to which she had readily succumbed. And through this dream-like state of perfect calm had drifted the conviction that the old life would no longer satisfy her; she yearned to live close to nature, to enjoy over and over again the wonders of sunrises and sunsets, the miracle of an African sky where the stars seemed to hang low in the cool purple dome of the heavens. She recalled having said to Flint, on their very first meeting, that here one could live one's life as nature ordained it to be lived. People like Flint and Mark were among the world's most fortunate beings, she decided. For them there was no rush, no real urgency, no avaricious notions that money is essential to happiness.

These thoughts, gradually intruding into her tranquillity of mind, only served to increase her own longing for a complete change in her way of living. She knew a tinge of envy as she dwelt on Kirsty's life, and how different it was from the one she had lived before marrying Mark and settling at Gimbulu Farm. Like her cousin, Kirsty had worked in an office, following a set routine which carried her from Monday morning to Friday afternoon. On Saturday and Sunday she would be cleaning up her flat, cooking, washing and ironing. There would be shopping, and any other chores to which she might decide to give her time. Liane's life was similar, though more hectic, for Richard was a far more energetic boss than the one by whom Kirsty had been employed.

'Hi! Did you have an enjoyable walk?' Kirsty's light inquiring voice greeted Liane as she reached the stoep, putting an end to her reflections. She glanced up with a smile and said yes, her walk had been very enjoyable indeed.

'I saw some wonderful sights,' she added enthusiastically as she joined her cousin, who was standing by the french window which opened out on to the front stoep. 'I walked along the river bank for the most part. It was beautiful!'

'Mark and I sometimes take that path. We love it.'

Voices came to Liane just as she was about to speak.

Flint and Mark were in the room behind, talking about crops. They emerged as Liane sat down, and Mark excused himself and went off to speak to one of his boys who was busy in the vegetable garden.

'Hello, Liane,' greeted Flint casually. 'You've been walking, Kirsty tells me. Did you enjoy it?' His dark grey eyes roved over her and it was only then that she realised how dusty and dishevelled she must be.

'Very much,' she answered, leaning back in her chair. 'There's something new to discover every time I go out.'

'Liane—Flint, can I get you a cup of tea?' interposed Kirsty in a gay and happy tone. 'Or you might like something stronger?' Her glance was directed towards Flint, who was appearing undecided as to whether or not to stay.

'I'll have tea, please, Kirsty,' he said at length.

'Sit down, then. I shan't be long. I've to make it myself because Sylvester's not too well and I've made him go to bed.'

Liane was frowning slightly; she had no desire to be alone with Flint. He realised this and said, a sardonic edge to his voice,

'Your cousin did assure you that she wouldn't be long. However, if you would like me to take a short stroll in the garden until she returns I'm very willing to oblige.' His eyes taunted, his mouth was curved in a half-smile that denoted amusement mingled with a hint of contempt. Liane, flushing with embarrassment, knew that he was thinking about that interlude when she had so readily responded to his lovemaking.

'I see no reason why you should,' she managed, successfully injecting a careless note into her words. 'I'm quite happy to—er—chat with you.'

The amused smile deepened. He glanced at a vacant chair, decided not to take possession of it but instead stood casually with his back to the open window, sardonically watching her, his arms folded.

'I doubt very much that you're happy,' he remarked. 'Most certainly you're uncomfortable.'

Liane's colour deepened, but again she managed to keep her voice light.

'You take much for granted,' she said.

'I can feel your discomfiture, Liane—every time you find yourself alone in my company.'

Fleetingly she pondered this.

'I suppose it's natural that I should be that way.' It amazed her that she and Flint could converse like this, about something which had affected them both most strongly, although in different ways.

'There's no reason at all why you should feel uncomfortable,' he said. 'It's over and done with——'

'It isn't,' she broke in. 'Not inside me. I feel so ashamed, allowing myself to be carried away like that.' She turned from him and sat, tugging at the corners of her handkerchief. 'You must regard me with contempt —in fact, you reveal contempt very often.'

Flint made no denial; he continued to watch her, teetering forward on his toes, his hands now thrust into the pockets of his denims.

'You're a fool,' he pronounced unexpectedly. 'Do you not realise that frustration and regret could hem in your whole existence?'

She turned her head, startled, and her hands became idle in her lap. This was plain speaking indeed ... and yet she experienced no resentment that he should be so outspokenly familiar with her. It seemed neither wrong nor strange. And it was the same as regards his censorious expression, for it seemed in no way out of place. Liane recalled how, in that glade, she had felt weak and feminine; she felt the same at this moment and now, as then, the sensation was extraordinarily pleasant. She spoke at last, aware that Flint was waiting for her to make some response to what he had said.

'You're referring to—to the way I—I feel about my —employer?'

'Your unrequited love,' he said with a sort of brutality that made her flinch. 'Yes, I am referring to that.' His eyes held hers, cold and hard beneath their hooded lids. 'How long are you intending to cherish hopes that can never crystallise?' he queried with a hint of satire.

Mechanically she shook her head.

'I don't want to talk about it,' she quivered. 'It's my own private affair——'

'More often than not it does one good to talk about one's troubles. Evasion is easy but unproductive. Have you discussed the matter with your cousin?'

'Not fully.' Liane looked up into his set face, her blue-green eyes wide and appealing. 'Please don't press me, Flint,' she begged, speaking as if to someone who had been her friend for years. 'You don't understand.'

The grey eyes flickered. And as she watched their changing expression she became less confident that he did not understand.

'You would be better off if you left your employment,' he said after a pause. 'My words are more than advice,' he went on. 'They're protective.'

She said huskily,

'You're very kind, Flint, but Richard's reliance on me is so great that I couldn't leave him.'

'You'd like to?'

'I—think so.' She glanced away, her attention caught by the changing light as the sunset spread draperies of gold to adorn the distant girdle of hills. Some of Mark's boys, having finished their work in the fields, were slowly making their way towards the cluster of thatched huts that formed the settlement in which they lived with their wives and children.

'What you want,' said Flint tautly, 'is a darned good shaking!'

'Oh!' was all Liane could find to say to this incredible remark.

'Or perhaps some stronger treatment. Most certainly you need some common sense knocking into you.'

Liane felt a sharp tug of anger.

'I've said it's my own affair. I can't think why you should be so interested!' Where was her cousin? she wondered. Why was she taking so long over the tea?

Flint appeared not to be in any way affected by Liane's anger as he responded calmly,

'At your age you should have powers of easy resilience.'

'Well, it would appear that I haven't,' she almost snapped.

'I'd be ashamed to make such an admission.' His manner was still calm, a circumstance which made Liane feel inferior. This in turn caused her to look critically at him. He had that natural dignity which enabled him to appear immaculate even in casual dress. In fact, the white cotton shirt and the dark blue denims seemed, if anything, to accentuate that high-bred look which was always so much a part of him, and which made him so outstandingly attractive. His hands were resting on the back of a chair and her eyes were drawn to them. Strong, capable hands, the fingers long, firm yet flexible, and very brown. He moved, coming round to sit on the chair, a sort of mild amusement in his hooded eyes. Liane caught her breath involuntarily, aware of that quickening in her veins which she had experienced before when she was alone with Flint. No use even trying to ignore what was so obvious, what she had discovered before now—that she was by no means unaffected by the distinctive and manifold attractions of Flint Dawson.

Aware of her observation, Flint gave her a quizzical look; she felt the colour tint her cheeks, and turned her head away. The great fiery ball of the sun was falling rapidly behind the faraway hills and its long slanting rays, dancing through the wind-teased foliage of the tamarisk trees bordering the lawn, burst into a thousand reflections as they touched the ground. Another miracle of nature! She could never tire of such magnificence, not if she witnessed it a million times.

'What are you thinking, Liane?' The voice, almost gentle in its intonation, was like a caress and she brought her gaze to his.

'I was admiring the sunset,' she told him, her own voice soft and musical, and a trifle sad. This latter did not escape him and his brows contracted in a frown.

'You're thinking that, very soon, you'll be seeing our African sunsets for the last time?'

She nodded, noticing that there was no tautness about him this time, as her departure was mentioned, by Flint himself. Obviously he was already getting over his love for her. But then hadn't he just a few moments ago implied that it was futile to waste one's time and thoughts on love that was unrequited? He had said quite firmly—and imperiously, she now reflected—that she needed some common sense knocking into her. Well, Flint himself was not lacking in common sense. With resignation he was accepting the clear fact that she could never return his love, and therefore he was intending to forget that he had ever loved her ... and perhaps turn to someone else? Liane found herself in a strange state of confusion, impatient because the very idea of Flint's loving someone else seemed to jar on her emotions. Yet it had not always been so. She had up till now experienced only indifference regarding Flint's future; it mattered not one jot to her whom he married, or even if he chose to remain a bachelor.

He was regarding her with a look of inquiry at this moment and she realised that he was waiting for her comment.

'I was, in a way, thinking that there were few African sunsets left for me to see. But what I was really saying to myself was that I would never tire of such beauty, even if I saw it a million times.'

His grey eyes regarded her contemplatively.

'You could come here and live with Kirsty and Mark,' he said. 'I know they'd be delighted to have you.'

'Has Kirsty been talking to you?' inquired Liane a trifle indignantly.

Flint shook his head.

'Not openly about you,' he replied. 'But your cousin is very transparent, Liane. It doesn't take much endeavour to read between the lines when she's expressing her mind about anything.'

Liane was silent, feeling in some way that this situation was no less unreal than the one in which she found herself on that most intimate occasion in her glade. She was not now experiencing any embarrassment at all, even though Flint was making no attempt to curb his tongue concerning her own unhappy state. These latest admissions of his proved beyond doubt that he was aware of the invitation extended to Liane by her cousin to sell up and move out here permanently.

'I expect,' she murmured after a long pause, 'that your personal advice would be for me to leave England and settle out here?'

Not by a flicker of an eyelid did he betray any sign of emotion as he answered,

'That most certainly *is* my advice, Liane. In my opinion you're throwing away your future for this man whose only interest in life is the making of money——Yes, I say this at the risk of arousing your anger,' he said, noticing the sudden glint of resentment that came into her lovely eyes. 'He's engaged to be married, and if you would only spend a few moments of your time on a forcible and convincing introspection you'd come out of it overwhelmingly thankful that it's not you to whom he decided to become engaged.'

Already she was shaking her head to negate what he was saying. Her words amplified her thoughts as she said,

'I'd be the happiest woman alive if I were engaged to Richard.'

Silence, long and fraught with tension. Flint was

angry; it was revealed in the hardness of those dark grey eyes. Yet his anger was tempered by understanding, as was proved by his saying,

'You think you would, Liane, but it would be a transient dream and, believe me, the awakening would be more than a little painful.'

'You believe that I'd make a failure of my marriage?'

'To him, yes.'

She fell silent but looked at him. She saw the trace of a smile touch his lips before he said, the merest hint of sardonic amusement in his voice,

'Don't get the mistaken idea that I'm just saying these things out of—er—spite. I'm not that kind of man. I've accepted your word that you could never marry me, and even should you decide to come over here to live I should never trouble you in that way, so any apprehension you might have on that score is, I assure you, groundless.'

Calm as she had tried to be up till now, Liane was certainly put out of countenance by his latest speech, and an actual sigh of relief rose to her lips as Kirsty, attired in a dainty but totally inadequate little tea-apron, came on to the stoep carrying a tray.

'I'm sorry I've been so long,' she said rather breathlessly. 'I couldn't find anything! So much for being out of practice. I've been thoroughly spoiled since becoming the wife of an African farmer.' Her eyes had passed with a sort of shrewd observation from Liane to Flint and then back again.

'If I didn't know it was impossible I'd suspect you two of quarrelling.'

Flint laughed briefly.

'We haven't quarrelled, I assure you.'

126

After putting down the tray Kirsty straightened up, looking into his face.

'Have you been subjecting my cousin to one of your cutting lectures, then? I remember your giving me one —and I felt as uncomfortable then as Liane appears to be now.'

More plain speaking! Where was the tact which these two should have been practising?

'Shall I pour the tea for you?' Without waiting for an answer Liane picked up the cream jug. 'We all take milk,' she said to herself as she poured some into each cup. 'Is Mark not joining us?'

'No. Some minor mishap's keeping him, so we'll not wait.' Kirsty sat down, then passed a plate of home-made scones across to Flint.

'Do you mind if I don't have one?' he said. 'Aunt Miriam fusses so if I don't consume a massive dinner. She never will realise that a full-grown man requires less food than a growing boy.'

'She might fuss, but she's nice,' declared Kirsty. 'How long before she leaves?'

'She hasn't made up her mind.' Flint stretched out his long legs and took the tea from Liane. Leaning back in his comfortable chair, he regarded her over the rim of his cup, his expression veiled. Liane lowered her lashes, thinking suddenly of Alma, and of Aunt Miriam's opinion of her. She could not help speculating on the possibility of Flint's marrying her—not on the rebound, for, as Liane had said to his aunt, he possessed far too strong a personality to do anything so impulsive and irrational. But he might come to love Alma. After all, he was getting along with her very well until Liane herself had put in an appearance. Flint was obviously

127

philosophical about the non-fulfilment of his hopes in that direction, and it did seem that both his disappointment and his loss of pride were no longer on his mind. Lifting her eyes, she sought his face, and found him looking straight at her. She saw the gravity disappear from his eyes, dispelled by the hint of mocking amusement that entered into them.

'Just take a look at that scene!' Kirsty, about to sit down, made the exclamation and returned to the rail by which she had been standing while Liane poured the tea. 'We never had such sunsets in England!'

Both Liane and Flint looked towards the west, to where the refulgent tongues of flame spread in a vivid arc above the horizon, while the molten cloud reflections created a rosy veil with which to drape the drowsy landscape. Even as they watched, every trace of azure left the sky, replaced by orange and green and saffron-gold.

A tiny sigh escaped Liane involuntarily and a strange sense of unrest enveloped her. Flint, having transferred his gaze from the sunset to her face, inquired of her what was the matter.

She shrugged helplessly.

'I don't know,' she answered with another small sigh. 'I expect I'm feeling unsettled now that my departure is so close.'

Kirsty turned from her contemplation of the painted sky and looked down at her.

'Must you go, Liane?' Her voice was gentle and persuasive. 'Both Mark and I would love you to stay a while longer.'

'My holidays extended only to six weeks, Kirsty. I shall have to go.'

'Richard's managed without you all this time. He can manage another week or two.'

Liane shook her head.

'He told me, on the day I left, that he would be happy indeed on the day I returned to the office.'

Something akin to a sneer curved Flint's mouth, but he made no comment.

'He's put on you right from the first,' stated Kirsty, uncaring that Liane was sending her a pleading glance. 'I wouldn't care if he'd ever showed appreciation——'

'He does show appreciation,' interrupted Liane indignantly. 'I've told you what he pays me. And also there are the wonderful trips abroad that I get. All my expenses are paid, and it's first class travel and accommodation.' She was avoiding Flint's regard, but knew he was listening with interest to the interchange going on between her cousin and herself.

'I admit he pays you well,' said Kirsty, 'but what about the extra hours you work? As for the trips abroad—well, he could scarcely expect you to foot the bills for expenses, could be?'

Liane said nothing, and a few minutes later she was relieved to hear Flint say that it was time he was going.

'I'll be seeing you all at the *braaivleis* tomorrow evening,' he said finally. 'Come early if you like and we'll have a sundowner before the main fun begins.' He nodded to Kirsty, looked with an unreadable expression at Liane, and then, taking the steps with a light spring, he was gone from the stoep, into the silence of the garden. Kirsty, having already gathered the crockery on to the tray, picked it up and disappeared through the french window into the house.

Liane rose and stood by the rail, her eyes following

Flint's tall arresting figure until it was lost to view among the trees. The sun had sunk below the horizon now, but the hills were still spangled with fire. Frogs began to croak, mingling their unmelodious sounds with those made by the cicadas; from somewhere in the gathering twilight came the sharp aroma of some mountain herb, to meld deliciously with the pervasive scent of flowers growing in Kirsty's garden. Beyond this garden lay Mark's fields, purple and silent, with all the boys gone to join their families. And farther on still stretched the bush, motionless and quiet in that mysterious glow that precedes the onset of night. Gone now were the sepia hillsides, swept into the pools of shadow that robbed them of their identity.

The sound of a car engine caught Liane's attention and she allowed her eyes to wander to the end of the drive; she saw the red tail-lights of Flint's station wagon as they came round the curve, then they disappeared as Flint turned into the road.

All was hushed again and from over the rim of the earth came a blood-red moon, rising into the majestic vault of the sky, with one lone star for company. Dusk, diminishing rapidly, had given way to night.

# CHAPTER EIGHT

LIANE awoke to a room filled with sunshine; drowsily she realised she had missed the spectacle of dawn. And there would be only two more dawns for her to witness. How swiftly the six weeks had gone by! And yet, looking at it from another angle, she was admitting that it seemed an age since she had said goodbye to Richard in his office. Vaguely she had cherished the hope that he would miss her so acutely that he would at last see her true value ... but not merely as his secretary.

No chance, she thought practically as she slid from the bed. Marlene had been strengthening her position for some time, and now her place in Richard's scheme of things was firmly established.

Slipping on a dressing-gown, Liane went into the bathroom and turned on the water. While it was running she went over to the window. The familiar sight of the boys working in the fields met her eyes. They were singing; it did her heart good to know that they were happy. She recalled her feelings when, as a girl of about fourteen years of age, she had read *Uncle Tom's Cabin*, and cried bitter tears over the situation of the slaves—men like these who had been uprooted from their environment to be sold to the highest bid-

der. But those men out there were free, and in consequence, they were happy. Liane's thoughts turned in,
on to herself. She had admitted that she could be happy
here; she had on several occasions allowed her mind to
dwell fleetingly on the idea put forward by Kirsty—
and more recently by Flint—of settling here. She
would have to sell up, but she could envisage no problems there. She would have to resign her most enviable
position as private and confidential secretary to one
of the most prosperous businessmen in London. She
shook her head as, turning, she made her way to the
bathroom.

She would never leave Richard of her own accord.

Kirsty was in the kitchen with Sylvester when Liane
emerged from her bedroom. She stood by the open
door, looking in as her cousin stood at a well-scrubbed
table slicing bread.

'Is Sylvester better?' asked Liane just as he went
from the kitchen to the larder.

'He says he is, but I'm not convinced,' replied
Kirsty. 'That's why I'm helping with the breakfast. It's
so difficult,' she added not without humour, 'to tell
whether one of his kind is looking pale or not.'

'Missus,' came the voice of Sylvester from the
larder, 'I am not feeling pale.'

'You wouldn't admit it if you were,' she rejoined,
trying to look stern. 'I think you must go and rest.
Lulu will be here directly and she'll see to the breakfast dishes.'

The houseboy seemed to sigh, but even Liane, in-
experienced as she was with the African, could see
that he was not enjoying his usual health. After a pause

the boy shrugged resignedly and said yes, he would go and rest in bed.

'I shall make him stay there for the remainder of today,' Kirsty was saying as she and Liane sat over their breakfast, Mark having had his very early, before going out to the fields. 'If he's no better in the morning I'm having the doctor.'

The day passed pleasantly, the cousins going off in the runabout to do some shopping in Ravensville during the morning. They lunched at the smaller club, the Assegai, where there was a restaurant which was less expensive than that of the Sunset Club. Immediately after lunch they drove to the other side of town, where they both had appointments at the hairdressers, for that evening was the occasion of Flint's *braaivleis*.

Dress being casual, Liane wore well-pressed slacks of slate grey and a turquoise roll-necked cotton sweater, her only accessory being a Victorian fob watch on a fine chain, both of gold. Entwined in the exquisite engraving on the back of the watch were the initials: A.J. and Liane had often mused on who had owned the watch, what the initials stood for, and what the person was like. Liane had bought the watch at a little 'junk' shop, having espied it in the window, lying among a mass of worthless bric-à-brac. The chain had come later, after much searching around the antique shops and market stalls.

'As usual,' said Kirsty when they were both ready, 'you look very attractive.'

'Thank you,' responded Liane with a smile. 'So do you.'

'You like my flared pants, then?'

'Of course. They're all the fashion in England.'

133

'So I've heard. I bought these in Pretoria. Mark took me there a couple of months ago, to meet some friends of his.' Kirsty paused a moment. 'I love this blouse, and feel a proper swell in it! But I wonder if I ought to have a cardigan handy. What do you think?'

'The blouse is of fine wollen material and should be warm, but we do know that the evenings can become cold. Yes, I'd take a cardigan if I were you.'

Kirsty went off to fetch the cardigan and Liane glanced in the mirror to take one last look at herself. Her bright russet hair had been styled beautifully by the hairdresser in Ravensville and Liane decided it had never looked more attractive. Her skin, devoid of make-up, had a healthy tan, and her lips were rosy red. She knew she looked very young, and desirable ... and her thoughts flew to Richard. Yes, his image blotted everything else in her life at this moment. If she could have been granted one wish, it would be that he could see her now, in this pretty setting of the hall at Gimbulu Farm.

'Something wrong?' was Kirsty's instant inquiry as she returned with her cardigan in her hand. 'You look sort of—sad.'

'Sad?' Liane made an effort to shake off her dejection. 'I'm not sad, Kirsty.'

'Looking forward to the barbecue?'

'Very much.'

'Flint certainly knows how to entertain, doesn't he? But then he has the wherewithal to do it—an excellent cook, a house that will hold twenty people easily, gardens that will hold ten times that number, and of course, he has the money. There's never any stinting when Flint Dawson gives a party.'

'He seems to enjoy entertaining.'

'Yes, that's the impression I myself have always had. But it would be better if he had a wife, don't you think?'

'He might eventually marry Alma.'

'Heaven forbid!' Kirsty frowned as she spoke. 'Mark's sure he won't, but Alma's tenacious. She never strays far from him when they're at a party or any other function.' She paused to glance at her wristwatch. 'I expect Mark'll be ready for us now. Let's go out to the station wagon.'

Mark wasn't there, but as they were expecting him any moment they got into the station wagon and made themselves comfortable in the back. Several minutes passed, and still there was no sign of Mark.

'I think I'd better see what's keeping him,' said Kirsty, signifying with a slight frown that a tinge of anxiety had entered into her. 'He knows I wanted to be early, so that we could have that sundowner Flint mentioned, before the other guests arrive.'

Liane watched her slim figure until it disappeared into the house. Another wait ensued and Liane was just about to follow her cousin when Kirsty came running towards the vehicle.

'Sylvester's ill,' she told Liane. 'I'm staying with him while Mark goes for the doctor. Will you go on alone and tell Flint what's happened? We'll be along later——'

'Is there nothing I can do?' broke in Liane. 'Is he very bad?'

'Seems to be,' answered Kirsty on a troubled note. She then went on to say that Liane could not do anything if she stayed behind with her. 'Sylvester's lying

135

quite prone and I'm very sure he won't move. You go on, Liane. Take the runabout——'

'I can walk over the fields,' Liane began, then she remembered the heavy downpour they'd had that afternoon while she and Kirsty were in the hairdressers. 'It'll be muddy,' she added just as Kirsty was about to say the same thing.

'Take the runabout,' said Kirsty again. 'Ah, here's Mark, so I'll go and stay with Sylvester.'

Liane slid from the station wagon and Mark got in at once. There was no waste of time and within seconds he was out of the drive and turning into the road leading to Ravensville.

Flint was in the garden when Liane drove the runabout along his wide, tree-lined drive and stopped in front of the imposing façade of the homestead. He had been standing very still, looking across towards the fountain and the pool. On hearing the runabout he turned, a look of surprise as he saw Liane was on her own. Swiftly he came towards her, anxiety taking the place of his surprise.

'What's wrong?' he wanted to know before giving her time to speak.

She explained, adding that Kirsty and Mark would probably be along later.

'Will there be someone to stay with Sylvester?' he asked.

'I imagine Kirsty means to get Lulu—or perhaps one of Mark's boys.'

'I'm sorry to hear he's ill,' frowned Flint. 'Have you any idea what's the matter with him?'

Liane shook her head.

'He wasn't well when you were at Gimbulu yesterday,' she reminded him. 'But we didn't think it was anything really serious.'

'Is he feverish?'

'Kirsty says he's just lying there, very still.'

Flint was silent for a while; Liane knew that he was worried about the houseboy. Just another manifestation of his attractive personality, she thought. He could spare the time to be troubled over a servant who wasn't even his own.

'I feel I should go over and take a look at him,' said Flint at last. 'It will be some time before the doctor can be brought, even if he's at home when Mark gets to his house. Yes,' he added with decision, 'I'll go over and see if there's anything I can do.' He asked if Liane would care to remain behind, but went on to say that she would be on her own, as his aunt had decided to take a rest before the *braaivleis* began, and she was at present in bed. 'You can come back with me to Gimbulu, if you like?' he ended, and Liane agreed, not wishing to remain here, at his house, on her own.

His eyes had taken in her appearance and mingling with his anxiety over Sylvester was the undisguised admiration which by now was very familiar to Liane and which always resulted in her wishing it were Richard whose eyes were filled with admiration.

They went in the runabout, with Flint driving, on Liane's suggestion, as she felt he would be mentally finding fault with her driving if she took the wheel. The sun was dipping low on the horizon; shadows encroached on to the bamboo thicket just beyond the gate to Flint's house and it took on a grotesque appearance. Blue-gums on the roadside looked eerie and

137

gaunt, but the ubiquitous drought-resisting peppers fringing the opposite side of the road caught the lovely deep golden rays of the dying sun and took on an enchantment that was as wondrous as it was fleeting. After a while Flint said,

'Might I say how charming you look?'

She coloured in the dimness of the car.

'Thank you, Flint.'

'Very demure.' Sarcasm edged his tone as he spoke the two brief words.

'It's embarrassing to me when people remark on my appearance,' she rejoined with candour.

'I've always understood that females enjoy flattery.' Liane said nothing and he continued, 'You obviously have a flair for clothes and I'm sure you'd experience some disappointment if this flair went unnoticed.' Again she said nothing and Flint, after what seemed a moment of uncertainty, said in quiet tones, 'Perhaps there is only one person in whose eyes you want to be noticed?'

His words went home; she decided again on candour.

'Naturally I should be happy if Richard noticed me.'

'And flattered you?'

'Yes.'

'You're very honest, Liane.' His voice was cool, almost impersonal. Liane felt sure that he was not suffering any hurt because of her refusal to marry him. 'You have some attractive traits——' He slanted her a glance. 'I'm embarrassing you again, I suppose?'

'It doesn't appear to trouble you much,' she could not help retorting.

'It troubles me not at all,' was Flint's calm rejoinder.

'I find that with you I can say just whatever comes into my head.'

She looked at him in some surprise.

'I shouldn't imagine you were ever guarded. I mean, I suspect you always say what you want to say, regardless of whether people like it or not.'

He shook his head.

'I'm frank, yes, but I can also practise diplomacy if it should be necessary.'

'You never have with me, though.'

'That's what I've just said. I can say anything to you.'

He was trying to prove something, she thought perceptively. But what? She recalled having read somewhere the words: 'Between comrades there is nothing to hide.'

Was Flint of the opinion that their relationship was such that they were in fact comrades? Following this train of thought, Liane found herself saying,

'I, too, seem able to say what is in my mind.'

'That's what I meant just now when I commented on your honesty. You've spoken quite openly to me about this infatuation you have for your employer——'

'It is not infatuation!' she interrupted indignantly. 'It's lasted far too long.'

'You're right about its lasting far too long,' he returned bluntly. 'Anyone with any sense at all would have cut their losses long before now.'

'Richard happens to be my employer. Would you have me throw up my job?'

'It would have been the clear-headed thing to do,' he replied with a sort of heartlessness in his voice. 'But then a woman in love is never clear-headed, is she?'

'You appear to know a great deal about women?' she retorted, wondering—as on many previous occasions—just how she and Flint came to be conversing in this totally uninhibited manner. It had always been like this, so it did seem that they were comrades. Certainly there was something between them, something that could only be described as familiarity, since even politeness could go by the board, as was happening at this present time. 'Is it from experience?'

Flint gave a brief laugh and said,

'Most undiplomatic, my dear Liane.'

'But we've agreed that we can say just what comes into our minds.'

Again he laughed.

'Point taken,' he conceded. 'No, it is not from experience.'

Some inner force of curiosity made her want to talk about Alma, but even though this complete frankness characterised Liane's relationship with Flint, she found herself quite unable to broach the subject of the girl whom one day he might decide to marry. And so she fell silent, leaning back in her seat and staring ahead. Approaching nightfall had brought the bats into flight, their ghostly shapes borne on membraneous wings; from the African quarter across the veld could be discerned flickering lights—fires, probably, on which the evening meals were being cooked, while little naked piccanins stood by and watched, their big eyes round with interest.

Very soon the Gimbulu homestead came into view, identified by the waving crown of gum trees, dark now against the pearl-grey sky of early evening.

A few minutes later Flint was turning into the drive,

and within another few minutes he had surprised both Liane and her cousin by saying that Sylvester was in great pain.

'But he's so still,' protested Kirsty. 'How can he be in pain?'

'These people are stoics when it comes to suffering,' he returned grimly. 'I find their self-control and fortitude amazing.' He had brought some medical supplies with him and he opened the box, asking Kirsty to bring him two tablespoonsful of water in a glass. Into this he measured out some medicine and took it in to the sick man's bedroom. Liane and Kirsty, standing outside the door, heard Flint's soothing words as he helped Sylvester to a sitting position. There came another sound, that could have been a stifled moan, then Flint's encouraging,

'You must drink it, Sylvester. It'll ease the pain until the doctor arrives.'

The two cousins looked at one another, their lips quivering.

'I'd no idea he was in pain——' Kirsty turned away, swallowing convulsively. Liane's eyes were filling up; try as she would she could not prevent the tears from falling. Yet it was not totally for Sylvester that she wept. Within her some profound emotion was gaining strength, and she was in no doubt at all that it was Flint's kindness towards the African boy, his concern and compassion, that was so deeply affecting her. What a truly wonderful person Flint was! Expecting guests, and himself dressed for the occasion, he had not hesitated to come out here and tend the houseboy, easing his pain until the arrival of the doctor. Kirsty moved away and so it was Liane on whom Flint's eyes settled

141

as he emerged from the bedroom. His gaze became studied, and enigmatical.

'If you're ready,' he said without much expression, 'we'll be off. There's nothing more I can do for Sylvester. I believe he's suffering from poisoning of the stomach.'

Her eyes widened, allowing another tear to fall on to her cheek. Flint passed her his handkerchief without saying a word; she took it, dried her face and eyes, and handed it back to him.

'How has he been poisoned?'

'Eaten something. But the doctor's the best person to say.' His glance shifted as Kirsty returned. 'I'll have to go,' he said. 'My guests will be arriving soon now.'

'Thank you very much for coming, Flint. At least Sylvester isn't in pain now.'

It was still early and on their arrival back at Kimara Lodge they found that none of the guests had arrived. Nor was Aunt Miriam up yet, so Liane and Flint took their sundowner alone on the terraced verandah in front of the house. They were destined to be alone, she mused, trying to calculate just how often Flint and she had been together, without other company. He sat there, facing her, relaxing in the gay cotton-covered chair, his hooded eyes wandering over the garden to where a group of Africans—men and women—gossiped while waiting for his signal that the cooking could begin. This would be done on wrought-iron braziers which had been prepared, at intervals, under a long line of mahogany trees at the bottom end of the lawn. The fountain and pool were close by.

Lighted with multi-coloured lamps, the fountain looked like a scene from fairyland.

Kamau brought out drinks and a dish of tiny savouries made by Flint's gifted cook. Then the servant glided noiselessly away, his face and bearing as stolid as ever.

The evening was Turneresque, gentle, sublime, with a clear liquid glow still hovering in the west, as if it were determined to prolong the daylight. But over the implacable bushlands all was shadowed in the deep purple veil of twilight. Closer to, in the vague pools of darkness close to the grove of mango trees wherein lay Flint's summer-house, fireflies glowed luminous, like fairy lights being wafted about on a breeze.

Magic was in the very air around her, mused Liane, and as she turned her eyes towards her host she found herself saying, urged by some compulsion which she had no desire to resist,

'Flint, this is pure heaven—the wonder of it all ... I can't bear to leave it.'

He looked at her in silence, his mouth a little taut. Her eyes, wide and large, were limpid, her mouth soft and moving tremulously. She had no thought for Richard in this enchanting moment of unreality; Flint dominated the scene for her and there was in consequence no room for anyone else. His attractiveness, his magnetism and powerful personality—all these affected her mind and her senses, and even her heart, while all else—the atmosphere of an African night with its balmy air, its sights and its sounds—were but contributary to the sheer perfection of this trance-like state in which she found herself. Could there ever be another interlude just like this? Would she ever feel as she did now—happy and at peace, desiring nothing more than to be here, in the company of this most attractive man? He smiled, and she wondered what he would think were she to tell him how she was feeling.

'You can't bear to leave it,' he murmured at last, repeating her words softly to himself, almost, 'You have no need to, Liane.'

Something caught in the region of her heart. Was he still in love with her? Would he, on a little encouragement, repeat his proposal of marriage? And if he did propose could she, in the magic of this situation, trust herself to reject him? Startled by this train of thought, she tried to thrust it from her, only to be faced with the astounding, but unequivocal truth that, should there be such another scene between them as had occurred in her glade, she would, as she felt at this moment, eagerly consent to become his wife.

Did he still love her? she asked herself again. More important: what were her feelings for him? It was no use trying to bring Richard's face into her mental vision. It seemed not to matter at all if she never saw his face again. Wonderingly, bewilderedly, Liane attempted to bring order to her confused mind, to analyse these new and exciting sensations that were affecting every nerve in her body.

'Flint!' Suddenly, like the loud shattering of a piece of glass, Alma's voice broke into her thoughts and she actually gave a start which caused the tumbler in her hand to jerk and spill its contents on to her lap. 'Am I early for once, darling?' Alma came seductively up the steps and took the chair which Flint, having risen, offered to her.

'You're early, but not too early. What would you like to drink?'

'I'd like a Hawaiian,' she replied, her eyes straying to Liane in an all-examining glance which seemed to hold contempt. 'I expect this will be your last party? I hear you're leaving the day after tomorrow?'

'Yes, that's right.' Liane spoke politely enough, but her attention was with Flint who was going into the house to mix Alma's drink himself. She disliked the girl intensely, never having met anyone so rude as she, and sincerely hoping she never would again.

'Where are Kirsty and Mark?' Alma glanced around rather vaguely. 'Strolling in the romantic darkness,' she added with a sort of derisive amusement. 'Anyone would think they're still on their honeymoon.' A laugh escaped her as she opened her handbag and took out a gold cigarette case.

'Kirsty is my cousin,' said Liane pointedly and with an edge of ice to her tone.

'Sorry; I didn't mean to scoff,' returned Alma lightly. 'Cigarette?' The case was held out to her, but Liane said no, she did not smoke. 'You should try one,' advised the other girl. 'They soothe your nerves.' Extracting a filter-tipped cigarette she put it into a long holder.

'I don't require anything to soothe my nerves,' said Liane coldly.

'You're fortunate.' There was a slight drawl to the husky voice which could, thought Liane, be the result of boredom. 'Most people suffer from nerves these days.'

Liane said nothing. She did not even feel inclined to inform Alma that Kirsty and Mark were not strolling

145

around Flint's gardens, but were concerning themselves with one of their African servants.

'Your drink, Alma. I hope you enjoy it.'

'If it's made properly, darling, I shall.'

'It has the right ingredients.'

'Gin, orange-juice and curaçao,' murmured Alma, holding the glass to her nose. 'With ice.'

The cigarette was unlighted and Flint, picking up the lighter which matched the gold case, snapped it on. In its flame Alma's eyes, dark and beautiful, were concentrated on Flint's face, and suddenly Liane felt left out, alone and unwanted here. An alluring smile followed the deep inhalation of smoke after Alma had drawn on her cigarette, a smile that revealed, as always, those perfect white teeth and the tip of a small pink tongue. Flint's eyes were soft as they looked into hers, and a smile that was almost tender curved his mouth. No doubt about it, mused Liane, they made an arresting couple. One day in the not too distant future, they would surely marry. For it did seem that Flint was attracted to Alma, and as Liane watched them together she could not help suspecting that Flint's feelings for herself had been no more than infatuation. He certainly was not displaying regret; on the contrary, he always appeared to be happy and contented, and Liane fell to wondering if he were now grateful that she had rejected his offer of marriage. Alma, subtly flirting with him, invariably managed to bring forth a laugh or a smile, and when her drink was finished—rather quickly, Liane thought—he immediately went off to refill her glass.

'This time next week you'll be hard at work, I suppose,' commented Alma, regarding Liane through narrowed eyes.

'I shall, yes.'

'I'd hate to be cooped up in an office all day.'

'You'd get used to it, if you had to.'

Alma shrugged her elegant shoulders and pulled on her cigarette. Her eyes were fixed on the fob watch, and Liane strongly suspected that she was comparing it with the beautiful and expensive cocktail watch she herself was wearing. Small and dainty, it was studded with tiny diamonds, and it had a diamond clasp. Embellishing the smart white trouser suit she wore was a diamond clip which was fixed to one of the lapels.

'Will you ever come here again?' inquired Alma after a space.

'One day, I suppose. But it will be in the far distant future.' Liane glanced up, to meet Flint's eyes as he appeared at the table with Alma's drink. 'It's an expensive trip, and also one needs to have the time.'

'How drear—not to be mistress of your own time.'

Liane had no patience to continue the conversation and she fell silent, sipping her drink. Presently she heard Flint say, in that quietly modulated voice she now knew so well,

'What about your glade, Liane? Aren't you going to want to visit it from time to time?'

She coloured slightly, while Alma turned her head abruptly to send Flint an interrogating glance. She spoke before Liane had time to answer Flint's question.

'Glade? What's all this?'

'Liane owns one tiny piece of Africa,' said Flint. 'I gave it to her.'

Alma's expression underwent a staggering change.

Her eyes became hard, her mouth tight, and when she spoke her voice was almost harsh.

'You gave Liane some of your land, Flint?—made her a present of it?' Amazement mingled with the rising anger in her expression. 'I don't think I understand?'

Liane, becoming more and more uncomfortable, drained her glass and prepared to rise and leave the two together. Lights were flickering in the distance and she surmised they were from the cars of guests who would be arriving within the next few minutes.

'The glade bordering my forest,' Flint was saying pleasantly. 'We've called it Liane's Glade.'

'You've given her that?' Alma glanced at Liane, fury in her eyes. 'Whatever for?'

'She liked it,' was Flint's reply. 'Liane, your glass is empty. Can I get you another drink?'

She shook her head, aware of her heightened colour. Flint noticed it, and his eyes flickered strangely. There was something profound in the air; Liane sensed it, and, with dawning bewilderment, she found herself once again alone with Flint. Alma was as nebulous and unimportant as Richard had been a short while previously. There seemed to be a message in Flint's hooded eyes, and a certain tenderness in the slight curve of his lips. Alma, glowering at them in turn, noticed the bright gleam of Liane's russet hair, the alabaster skin and exquisitely-moulded features, the arched neck above sloping shoulders ... and hatred, dark and venomous, erased every other thought from her mind. Reflected in her eyes, this hatred was communicated to Liane on the instant and she shivered as a chill swept over her, bringing up the fine hairs on her forearms; she felt them rise beneath the sleeves of her sweater and automatically pressed her hands against them.

Flint frowned suddenly at the change in Liane's expression, and it was plain that he was puzzled. However, before he had time to say anything two cars, one closely following the other, swept round the wide curve leading from the road into Flint's drive and, excusing himself, he left the two girls to go and welcome his friends.

'I fail utterly to see why Flint should make you a present of that glade.' Alma spoke as soon as he was out of earshot. 'What good can it do you?'

Liane looked at her; the hatred still lingered in Alma's dark eyes.

'None, I suppose,' she replied, deciding she must be guarded as, after all, she was only a guest here, while Alma was a *favoured* guest.

'That glade,' submitted Alma, drooping her lids so as to hide her expression, 'is a favourite place for Flint and me. We go there in order to be quite alone ... and private.' A slight pause in order that this might sink in, and then, 'I expect Flint gave it to you because of the quarrel we had. He was terribly upset at the time—but he took the quarrel far too seriously, thinking I no longer cared for him.' Another pause ensued. Liane, taut and aware again of that chilling sensation, waited for the girl to continue, which she did, still hiding her expression by the lowering of her eyelids. 'I seem to remember his saying something about the glade having no meaning for him any more, and that he didn't think he would ever go there again. However, he must have done, because he showed it to you. And he gave it to you.' Alma looked straight at Liane now as she added, 'You can see for yourself the stupidity of his action. The glade's no good to you, is it?'

Automatically Liane shook her head. She had thought at the time that the gift could not do her any good, seeing that she would be living so far away from it. Yet the gift had thrilled her, for the glade was such a rare gem of natural beauty which no hand of man could create.

And it had been the place where Flint and Alma could be alone ...

Following on to this thought was the memory of Flint's proposal. Had he, after all, done what Liane had felt he could never do?—proposed marriage on the rebound? When this suggestion was put forward by Aunt Miriam the positions of Liane and Alma had been reversed and it was Alma to whom the old lady feared he might propose, having been rejected by Liane. Now, it would seem, it was Liane to whom he had turned after having had a quarrel with Alma.

Liane shook her head; she was still of the opinion that Flint was far too fine a man to stoop to anything so petty as that sort of revenge on Alma. Was Alma lying, then? If so, what was she expecting to gain?

'You're frowning,' commented Alma rudely. 'Something troubling you?'

Liane's mouth went tight.

'If it were,' she returned icily, 'it would be my own affair.'

'Oh!' The girl adopted an injured air. 'There's no need to be so unfriendly towards me.'

Liane said, rising to her feet,

150

'If you'll excuse me ...? I see someone I want to talk to.'

'Taken offence, have you?' Alma's voice had a supercilious edge to it. 'I've never met anyone quite so peculiar as you.'

Without a word Liane left her sitting there, and as Carl Van der Galt was at that moment disengaging himself from the company of his parents and sister, she went forward to meet him. His face lit up at her approach and he held out both hands to her in a friendly gesture. She gave him hers ... and at that moment Flint happened to come along, having just greeted the Bergers on their arrival. His eyes met Liane's; she noticed the hardness in them—and admitted to herself that it hurt. Turning away as he chatted with the Bergers, he did not even trouble to speak to Liane; and Carl, obviously aware of the sudden change in Liane's expression, asked if something were wrong.

'No, not at all,' she replied, managing a swift smile. 'Shall we go over and take a look at the food?'

'If it tastes as good as it smells ...' Carl sniffed and sighed. 'He's so darned lucky with those whom he employs. Still, one can understand why they do their very best for him. He treats them as equals, and he pays twice as much as anyone else.'

'I imagine he does pay his workers well.' She had seen his boys in the forest, and in the citrus plantations. They worked well and conscientiously, and Aunt Miriam had told Liane that never had there been any troubles on the Kimara estate.

The evening passed most enjoyably for Liane, much to her surprise, for although it had begun pleasantly—

when she and Flint were alone on the stoep—it had not been so promising when Alma appeared. However, Carl was good company; he kept close until Kirsty and Mark arrived, and after that the four were together for most of the time. Sylvester was very ill, but not dangerously so. The doctor had commented favourably about Flint's action in saving the man from any more unnecessary pain. Lulu was with Sylvester now, Mark said, but they did not mean to be too late in getting back to Gimbulu.

From time to time Flint would join the four, but Alma was never far away, a circumstance which disgusted Aunt Miriam, who herself kept joining them. She seemed not to be her usual cheerful self, but her dignified appearance remained with her, being inherent, thought Liane. So straight, the old lady was, and so distinguished in the way she walked. But every time she saw Alma she frowned.

'Why is Flint hovering around her like this?' she inquired of Liane when on one occasion she managed to get her alone. 'I can't think he cares for the creature —and yet ...'

Liane knew that it was Alma who was doing the 'hovering' but she naturally refrained from saying so. The fate of Alma and Flint was suddenly of no importance to her. For tomorrow she would be packing up, in preparation for her departure for home on the following day.

# CHAPTER NINE

RICHARD glanced up as Liane entered the office on her first morning back at work. She had knocked on his door, but had entered without waiting for his invitation, a practice which he had long since requested her to adopt.

'Ah, Liane!' The hard cold eyes of the businessman melted under the pleasure of seeing her again. 'Did you have a wonderful holiday?' He stood up, and they stared at one another across the sumptuously-appointed room.

'Yes, Richard, I did. Africa is a wonderful country.'

He nodded, and for a long moment he seemed overcome with emotion.

'You've been away for months,' he said.

She laughed, but it was not a happy laugh. She found no pleasure in being back in the office.

'Six weeks,' she reminded him, and again he nodded.

'It seems like months. Liane, I don't know how I've managed without you.' His voice was low and serious, his eyes still glowed with pleasure.

'But you *have* managed, Richard.' Liane came forward into the centre of the room and for a few seconds her gaze was fixed on the huge oak desk with its brass-handled drawers and inlays. She had been with him when he bought it—from Sothebys in London—and it had cost well over a thousand pounds. It was probably worth twice that much today, judging by the way antiques had shot up in value.

'Yes, I have managed,' Richard rejoined, 'but with the utmost difficulty. Never go away for so long again, Liane. Promise me.'

Something in his tone startled her, catching at her pulse so that it began to race.

'You've really missed me?' she asked, and he nodded without a moment's hesitation and answered, in a tone more mellowed than she had ever heard him use to her before,

'I've really missed you, my dear.' He seemed to swallow something hard in his throat. 'You haven't made me that promise,' he reminded her.

She hesitated, confused thoughts jostling about in her mind. She had spent the whole of the flight time from Africa in thinking about her future. And by the time the plane touched down at Heathrow Airport she had made her decision: she would leave Richard's employ and seek for a post elsewhere. She had no real ties, having put everything into her job and leaving herself little time for the cultivation of friendships. In fact, she had made more friends during her short stay in Africa than she ever had in her own country. Now, however, as she stood in the familiar office, looking into the face of the man she had loved for so long, she found herself once again pitched into a vortex of indecision. Never to see Richard again ...

And yet surely it would be worse to see him with his wife, to know that she herself was nothing more to him than the efficient robot which she had always been.

But would it be like that? Looking into his face, noting the anxious expression, the softness of the eyes and mouth, she began to wonder . . .

'How is Marlene?' she asked, abruptly changing the subject.

'Fine—fine. Liane, you haven't made me that promise.' His voice was insistent; she knew she must make up her mind immediately. But indecision still held her and she suddenly saw a way in which she could gain a little time.

'I shall never go on a six-week holiday again while I'm working for you,' she said with a smile.

'While you're working for me?' he repeated with a pucker of his forehead. 'I don't like the sound of that, Liane.'

'I shan't always be with you, Richard,' she told him practically. 'Changes take place in our lives, changes which affect us in various ways. I might one day decide to find a different kind of job altogether.'

The pucker became a frown causing deep creases between his eyes.

'I can't imagine being without you, Liane.' He shook his head and his mouth seemed to move spasmodically. 'I *can't* be without you.'

'Can't?' she quivered, her eyes glowing with optimism. 'You mean . . .?' She stopped, flushing with embarrassment. This was no intimate scene where she could urge him on to the point where he would propose marriage.

'I mean, Liane, that I've come to the conclusion that you're indispensable to me.' He seemed unsure of himself, and of her reaction to what he was saying—or rather, trying to say. Gone was the suave, confident tycoon. In his place was a man whose whole demeanour was one of pleading, and anxiety. 'It took me far too long to realise just how much I depended on you, dear. It's all been taken for granted, but while you've been away it's come to me just what I owe you.' He stopped and bit his lip. 'What I'm trying to say, Liane, is—is— that I would like to marry you.'

A deep and profound silence fell on the room after he had finished speaking. Liane, her heart beating far too quickly, was asking herself several questions at once, but the most important was: why hadn't she gone away before—left Richard on his own for six weeks, as she had done this time? What did it matter, though? The question she had waited so long to hear had been asked—not as romantically as she would have wished, nor in the setting she would have liked to remember in the years to come. But it had been asked for all that, and she had only to say yes, she would marry him. Instead, she spoke of Marlene, reminding him that he was engaged to her.

'I shall tell her it's all off——' Richard frowned, and Liane, knowing him as she did, could sense his feelings at the idea of going back on his word. 'Liane, dear, if you'll consent to marry me, then Marlene will have to take the break in the correct light—admitting that we weren't meant for one another.'

'She might be in love with you——'

'Might?' frowned Richard. 'I didn't think there was any doubt about that.'

'No,' murmured Liane, regretting her turn of phrase. 'No, of course not.' Liane turned away as she spoke, for she was very sure that Marlene's chief interest in

Richard was his money, and that he would not have been very long in finding this out.

'You haven't given me an answer, Liane.' His voice, lacking confidence as it did, seemed so wrong, for in any business deal he carried all before him, dominating every board meeting, influencing every transaction. His was the power behind the success of the firm, his the word that everyone held in awe.

Liane stood there, on the thick-pile carpet, wondering why she hesitated like this. She'd been in love with Richard for almost as long as she had worked for him; she had longed for this situation, and the question which had come at last. So why, she asked herself again, was she hesitating?

Suddenly, leaping into her consciousness, was that scene in her glade—Flint's passionate kisses, his strong arms embracing her, his tenderness and his words, 'Darling Liane, will you——?' She had stopped him, but these words of his had followed on after he had said he wanted her for his wife. Liane recalled how she had wished that it was Richard who wanted her for his wife. She had admitted to Flint that she would have been the happiest woman alive if she were engaged to Richard. Well, she could become engaged to Richard within the next few minutes; she only had to say the word. Instead of saying the word she was recalling so many incidents: her admission that she was not immune to Flint's attractions, her restlessness on that evening when Aunt Miriam had sent her to the summer-house with a message for him. She had admitted to herself that she could have stayed with him, that she *wanted* to stay with him. She had a vivid recollection of heightened emotions on several occasions

157

when she was alone with Flint; she remembered how the idea of his marrying someone else had jarred ... and yet she had ignored all these signs ...

Just what was she trying to tell herself——?

'Liane,' came Richard's voice breaking into her reverie, 'don't say no, dear. I've said I can't manage without you and I mean it. You know me well; you've met up with all my faults at one time or another. Surely you have no doubts about the future?'

'No, none.' She meant what she said. Richard could never be any other than a good husband, generous, clean-living, with an interest in his home.

'Well, then?'

Something made her say,

'Why do you want to marry me, Richard?'

'Because I can't be without you,' he answered. 'Haven't I just said so?'

Liane looked straight ahead, avoiding his gaze.

'You mean—in the office?'

He looked perplexed.

'I miss you here, yes——'

'And that's the reason for your wanting to marry me?' As she spoke he lifted a finger to halt her words, but did not manage to do so.

'Wait a minute, Liane!' His voice was stern and chiding. 'I want you for my wife because I need you in every way. Yes, you'll continue to help me with work problems, but you'll be the mistress of my home.'

She said quietly, marvelling at the calmness that had come over her,

'You don't love me, do you?'

He turned away; she was sure his face twisted— perhaps with regret. Certainly it was not with anger or annoyance at her words. Richard was never angry or annoyed with her.

'I must have some strong feeling for you, Liane,' he said at last. 'I missed you so much. Life seemed empty——'

'Marlene? Surely you went out with her—took her dining and dancing?'

'Sometimes, yes.' He was looking at her again. 'But all the while I had this sense of loss, of emptiness. There was no doubt in my mind, after the first fortnight or so, that your absence was at the root of the trouble.'

'I've been on holiday before.'

'Never for more than a week——' He stopped, looking pained. 'That was another thing, Liane. I kept on thinking how selfish I'd been, asking you to cancel holidays, to put off engagements, expecting you to give me all your time——'

'You didn't ask me to put off engagements, Richard.'

'All right. But I knew when you'd put one off, and I didn't care. The demands of my business were all that mattered and I never stopped to consider whether or not it was convenient for you to drop everything and come when I called, as it were. Twice I heard you on the telephone, cancelling an engagement, and I never gave the matter a second's thought. You cancelled holidays, and I've taken it as my right that you should put me first.' He looked at her with sincere apology in his eyes. 'I've been a blind fool, Liane, and there's no excuse I would dare to offer for my rank inconsideration. Brooding here, while you were away for so long, I fell to wondering how you could have stayed with me all this time. Any other girl would have found herself

159

another job, and it would have been only what I deserved.'

How frank and honest he was! His honesty and fairdealing in business had struck her from the start, awakening within her the admiration which had soon strengthened into love. Six years of loving him ... and now she could be his wife.

'I mustn't make a mistake!' The vehement exclamation escaped her unbidden, a secret thought which had escaped. Faintly bewildered, Richard looked inquiringly at her.

'That's a strange thing to say, Liane. You've just admitted that you have no doubts about the future.'

Her lovely eyes were moist as she said, in a low and husky tone,

'I must have time, Richard. At this present moment I can't think clearly; my mind's totally confused.' How incredible it was that she should be hesitating, floundering in a mist of uncertainty. During all those years of waiting and hoping for a moment like this, she had been so sure that if ever Richard's proposal of marriage did come, her answer, ready and eager, would be given with confidence and joy. Most certainly it would be given without a moment's hesitation.

'Yes,' he was saying, 'you must have time. I've sprung it on you, Liane. I didn't mean to, my dear, but it was just that I felt I needed the security which your answer would have given me.'

'You needed security?' Surprise edged her voice. 'You've always struck me as being very secure, and self-sufficient.'

'I can understand your gaining that impression,' he admitted after a thoughtful pause. 'But, Liane, men like me can be lonely; they can sometimes long for a prop—someone near and dear to lean upon. I need you, so please don't be too long in agreeing to marry me.'

She could not help saying,

'You seem confident that I shall say yes.'

'I'm hoping you will, Liane.'

She walked over to the window and looked down, into a thoroughfare packed with people shouldering their way on either side of four lines of traffic. Her thoughts took wings and she was on the stoep of Gimbulu Farm, enjoying the view of trees and fields, of the tawny veld where scattered bushes and wind-swept grasses of saffron and topaz stretched away to merge with the terracotta hills in the distance. She saw the willows by the river, the exotic flowers and fruits in Kirsty's garden. And she saw it all at night, moon-pale and still, with the air filled with the honey-scent of herbs and other vegetation.

A restlessness enveloped her; she wanted to shake it off, but it persisted. Turning around, she faced him once again. So big he was, broad-shouldered and powerful, with slightly greying hair and a large, good-tempered face.

'I'll think about it,' she promised. And then she said, wanting only to be honest, 'Africa did something to me, Richard. I loved the peace, the living close to nature. The people I met nearly all worked on the land; they seemed part of the great outdoors.' She hesitated, but only for a second. 'Kirsty asked me to consider going over and settling there. Neither of us has any other near relative.'

A heavy frown darkened on Richard's forehead.

161

'You'd never settle there, Liane,' he protested. 'You're too used to all that civilisation can provide.'

Her eyes flickered as she thought of the trips she had enjoyed with him.

'Plush hotels and people waiting on me? Is that what you mean?'

'Partly.' He glanced at her clothes. 'You'd not be able to dress like that.'

Suddenly there was a tinge of bitterness within her, caused by his remark about her clothes. For this was the very first time he had ever noticed what she was wearing.

'Perhaps I wouldn't want to,' she rejoined, wondering what he would say were she to tell him the truth—that she had deliberately acquired a dress sense in order to make him notice her.

'Please don't think of leaving me, Liane.'

'You—you need me?'

'I've already said so, my dear.'

Absently she nodded her head to signify that this had not escaped her.

'I'll think about your proposal,' she said again. 'It's not a decision I can make in haste.'

'I understand.' Richard's eyes were focused beyond her; he seemed to be staring unseeingly at the wall. Liane, aware of a tension in the air, making the long silence uncomfortable, found herself saying,

'Hadn't we better get down to work? I expect a great deal has piled up for me while I've been away?'

'Yes, it has,' he admitted, waking from his reverie. 'First will you type the letters which are already on the dictaphone? Then I want you to accompany me to lunch. I'm meeting the Chairman of Birtwistles and shall want you to make some notes.' The change in his demeanour was dramatic; he was again the brisk and efficient businessman, level-headed, calculating. His confidence flowed, his eyes took on that hard cool quality which was far more familiar to Liane than the gentle expression which had lingered in their depths so short a while ago. 'There's a board meeting to-morrow, and on Wednesday we shall be off to Paris, returning on Saturday evening. You won't mind work-ing on Saturday, of course?' A question, but his ex-pression told her that he was taking her agreement for granted. Something that could only be described as sadness caught at her heart. It would seem that they were right back where they had started.

For the whole of the morning Liane pondered over her situation, one moment managing to convince her-self that she wanted to marry Richard, but the next moment warning herself that it would never work out. She recalled vividly Flint's assertion that she would not make a success of marriage with Richard. Flint with his keen perception had known just how different they were in their outlook on life—with Richard almost obsessed with making money, and she loving nature and all things connected with it.

The idea of failure had not once crossed her mind in all those six years. Marriage to the man for whom she worked was the ultimate of her dreams; nothing could ever go wrong, for her love was such that it would always be a strong shield against all those disasters which beset marriages these days. She had no qualms about Richard's fidelity, and this confidence she still retained. But doubts were creeping in at an alarming rate, and for the very first time she was admitting that the rosy picture she had carried in her mind could be but the result of dreams rather than realities. Added to these doubts was the knowledge that Richard did not love her; this latter was of course contributary to her hesitation, but certainly not the real cause of it since she had always believed that she could make him love her, once they were married. Now, however, it was dawning upon her that his falling in love with her before marriage had always hovered somewhere in her scheme of things, and that she had hoped a proposal of marriage would be prompted by love, as it had been with Flint.

A proposal, she mused, should be romantic and she supposed that in her subconscious she had seen it like that, with Richard's lips close to hers, his arms about her. Instead, the proposal had been made in the cold atmosphere of the office, with Richard standing some distance from her, and without one tender word or kiss ever having been exchanged between them. No wonder she was hesitating!

Her mind protested and she saw herself as the poor, lovelorn creature at whom Flint had scoffed, telling her outright that she should long ago have cut her losses. Well, she could cut her losses now, and she would! Painful it might be, but she even had her doubts about that. A feeling of freedom was gradually creeping into her mind and her heart; it was as if a great weight was, mercifully, being lifted from her, allowing her to think more clearly, to extend her vision beyond this office and the big man who dominated it. Often she had convinced herself that he could not manage without her, but the past six weeks had proved that he could. No one was indispensable, and a replacement for her would be made without much difficulty.

All through lunch Richard seemed uneasy, repeatedly glancing at her as if he would have his answer now, reading it in her eyes. Liane remained indifferent, marvelling at the complete self-possession she was maintaining, for she had expected this lunch to be an ordeal, with her mind engaged in finding some gentle way of imparting the information that she was not going to marry him. After leaving the hotel they drove in silence, Richard at the wheel of his Mercedes, to the office. Liane went straight to her own room, worked steadily until five o'clock, then entered Richard's office. He glanced up expectantly, then rose and indicated that she should take the chair on the other side of his desk. She remained standing, pale but composed, and even now amazed that she could even contemplate refusing an offer of marriage from him.

'You've made up your mind?' He spoke first and she was glad; it provided an opening for her to say,

'Yes, Richard—and it's—no, in answer to your proposal of marriage.'

He started, his eyes staring unbelievingly.

'You haven't given yourself enough time, Liane, dear,' he began, when she interrupted to tell him she was leaving his employ. 'No——!' He shook his head as if the action could negate her decision. 'I won't accept it!' His voice quivered yet held the determination with which he conducted his business meetings. 'I refuse to accept your resignation!'

It was Liane's turn to stare, since she had never

165

heard him speak to her with such a harsh and angry note to his voice.

'You can't refuse to accept it,' she told him reasonably. 'You see, I've almost made up my mind to settle close to my cousin——'

'Africa's no place for you,' he cut in roughly. 'How are you intending to live? You can't let your cousin's husband keep you indefinitely.'

She opened her mouth to make a protest, then closed it again. Richard was so upset that he had no idea what he was saying.

'I can probably get a job,' she said quietly.

'Not like this one!'

'Over there you don't need much money.'

'You'll miss such a lot, Liane,' he said persuasively. 'Why won't you marry me? You haven't given me a reason, and there must obviously be one—for your refusal, I mean.'

She nodded, passing her tongue over lips that had gone dry. This scene was so sad; she never thought she would ever hurt him, or even go against his wishes.

'You don't love me,' she returned simply. 'That's the reason——' He was frowning heavily and she paused a moment. 'Love does happen to be important, Richard,' she added at length.

'I could soon learn to love you, Liane.'

'I doubt it.'

His large hands were clenched at his sides, and she noticed the spasmodic movement of a nerve in his throat.

'Have I given over too much of my life to making money?' he asked almost brokenly. 'I could have struck a happy medium, couldn't I?'

'Perhaps ...' Liane thought about this, then shook her head. 'You wouldn't be happy unless you were fully engaged in making money, Richard. I don't know why I haven't faced the truth before now. I've been a fool——' She stopped, but not quickly enough. She saw Richard's eyes widen, felt them fixed upon her face—perceptively even though they searched for something which he hoped to find there.

'You—love me,' he murmured wonderingly. 'Liane, my dear—how long——?'

'It's not important now.' Flushing hotly, she turned away, as if she would leave the office at once. 'I can't deny it because that would be dishonest. I've cared for you since—since ...' She found her voice failing her, because the tears were close, and because she was hurting him, but more than anything she wanted to weep for a lost love.

Yes, lost! She looked up into his rugged, handsome face, and knew she no longer loved him.

# CHAPTER TEN

Two months had passed since her return to Africa, two months of spring weather when the flowers bloomed with exotic profusion in the garden of Gimbulu Farm. It was now mid-December and Liane was settled in her post at the library. She had not yet fully made up her mind about staying in Africa permanently, but, as both Mark and Kirsty had said, there was no urgency for her to come to a decision.

'It's not inconveniencing us at all that you're here,' Mark assured her one evening when they were all on the stoep with their pre-dinner drinks. There had been a week of sultry white heat, and the breeze blowing in from the mountains was more than welcome, coming as the sun went down, and providing a cool and refreshing draught of pine-scented air which dispersed the still, humid atmosphere that had hung over the landscape since dawn. 'You can stay as long as you like.'

Liane smiled gratefully.

'It's good of you both,' she began, when her cousin interrupted her.

'We love having you, Liane, so don't be grateful. We only hope you'll stay for good.'

'If I do I must find a small place for myself.'

'Yes, of course,' from Mark as he leant forward to take up his glass. 'It's natural that you'll want your own home.'

Liane fell silent, her thoughts turning to Flint, as they invariably did when she was sitting here, with the long white homestead of Kimara Lodge visible through the trees. Lights were on in several windows, giving a most warm and welcoming aspect to the house.

Since her return the slow and gradual truth had come to her that her feelings for Flint were not merely those of friendship. Repeatedly she would live again that passionate and lovely interlude which had taken place in her glade, and the conviction would come to her over and over again that, had she stopped to examine her feelings earlier, she would have realised that she cared for Flint in a way that was totally different from anything she had felt for Richard. But instead of stopping to examine her feelings she had continued to be obsessed with the idea of her love for Richard; there was no room in her mind for the conception that she might be able to love another man. Richard was the one and only star in her heaven, and only now did she realise that her mind had been gradually becoming so narrowed that the whole of her thoughts and desires were centred on one person almost to the exclusion of everyone else. She had made no friends because she had permitted the demands of her job to isolate her, consuming all her time, absorbing all her energies.

And for what? There had been some appreciation from her employer, but no real display of gratitude. Yet Liane had not seemed to mind this, knowing as she did that the omissions stemmed only from thoughtlessness, since Richard's mind was invariably centred on making money.

'Liane, love, you're dreaming.' Kirsty's soft voice broke into her reverie and she glanced at her cousin across the rattan table.

'I'm not brooding, Kirsty,' she said, but not until Mark had gone into the house to fetch more drinks. 'So you needn't look so concerned.'

'You'll get over it, now that you're here.'

'I already have.'

'Truly?' with a widening of Kirsty's eyes.

'Truly. I'm not in love with Richard now.'

'It must be a relief!'

'Believe me—it is,' was Liane's heartfelt rejoinder.

Flint had once told her she ought to be glad she wasn't engaged to Richard—and she *was* glad!

The following afternoon Flint strolled into the library, went over to one of the shelves and chose a book, then brought it to the counter. Liane was alone, as it was the hottest part of the day and few people were out.

'You're not very busy.' The comment was as casual as it was smooth. Ever since her return his attitude towards her had been one of near-indifference.

'People don't come in much in the afternoons now.' Her voice was low, and friendly. 'It's so hot.'

Flint watched her stamp the front page of the book.

'What about you? Does the heat trouble you?'

'A little,' she admitted, pushing the book across the counter. 'I expect I shall get used to it, though.'

He ignored the book, his eyes on her face, a sort of piercing quality about his regard.

'You don't look one hundred per cent,' he said

abruptly. 'They ought to close the library between twelve and four.'

'But in that case I'd have to work until seven or eight o'clock. I'd rather put up with the heat and leave at five.'

The hooded grey eyes became expressionless.

'You know best what you prefer,' he said, picking up the book. 'Goodbye, Liane.'

His cool unemotional words were like a shower of cold water; she turned away even before he had reached the door. But she heard a feminine voice and twisted round again. Alma, looking incredibly cool and well-groomed, was standing at the entrance as Flint emerged, and they had met on the step.

'Darling! I didn't expect to see you! I surmised you'd be hard at it in your orange groves.'

'What are you doing out in all this heat?' asked Flint, bypassing her comment. 'You're going to ruin your complexion.'

Liane watched as the girl looked up into his face, a coy expression on her own.

'Would it trouble you, darling Flint?' drawled the husky voice.

Liane could not be sure whether or not Flint's eyes had flashed towards where she was standing, behind the wide wooden counter.

'But of course, Alma. You know very well that I've always admired your very lovely skin.'

It did seem to Liane that Alma's face registered surprise. However, the girl obviously enjoyed the flattery because she murmured cooingly,

'That's a charming thing for you to say to me, Flint.' And, after a slight pause, 'I see you've been in and

171

got a book. I was about to do the same. Will you wait for me?'

'I'll come in with you. Perhaps we'll go for some tea afterwards?'

'I'd adore that!' she purred. 'The Sunset Club verandah?'

'Fine.' Flint stood aside as Alma walked into the library, and if he noticed the arrogant, supercilious glance that was thrown in Liane's direction it affected him not at all.

'It'll be cool under the vines—— Have you noticed the lovely crimson flowers on those vines?'

'They're there every spring and summer,' he said.

While Alma was choosing a book Flint occupied his time in examining the paintings on the wall. Most of them had been there for some time, but noticing one in particular, he stopped abruptly and Liane heard him say,

'This is new——' He twisted round. 'Who brought this in?' he asked. 'There's no name on it.'

For a moment there was silence, and then Liane answered,

'A young woman put it there.'

'What young woman?' he frowned. Liane coloured; she had spoken without thinking that he knew all the young women for miles around. But she had not wanted him to know that it was hers. 'Whose is it?' he persisted when she did not speak.

Liane coughed to clear her throat.

'It's mine,' she returned briefly.

'Yours? You painted it?'

She smiled faintly.

'No, I couldn't paint like that. It was done by a

172

friend of my mother's, many years ago. This lady was very gifted, and several people who have seen the painting have said it will be valuable one day——' She broke off, shrugging lightly. 'I don't care about the value. I just love the way it's done—the way the trees blend with the sky, as if they're joined together, almost. In some aspects it reminds me of Watteau.'

'Just what I was going to say——'

'Oh, I don't think it does, Flint.' Alma looked frowningly at the large gilt-framed picture, which was of a parkland scene with water and people in flowing costumes sitting on long seats or moving about. 'I shouldn't think it'll ever be worth much. Now my Renoir——' She stopped on noticing the expression in Flint's eyes. 'I suppose one shouldn't boast about one's possessions,' she said, offering him a placatory smile. 'Come, I've chosen my book, so let's be off. I'm simply dying for that lovely afternoon tea you've offered to buy me!'

'You haven't given this to the library, I hope?' Flint looked at Liane, who immediately said no, she had merely lent it.

After stamping Alma's book Liane watched her and Flint leave the building, cross the courtyard with its waving palms and little flower beds in which grew anthurium lilies and allamandas, and a couple of gorgeously purple jacaranda trees, and get into Flint's big white car. Smoothly it left the park, and the short drive, to turn at the end and become lost to view.

Broodingly Liane sat down and rested her chin between her hands. Her mind persisted in presenting her with a picture of Flint and Alma, seated under the shade of the vines, on the broad verandah of the Sunset

Club. A dusky waitress would serve them, smiling to reveal a row of perfect white teeth.

'It's your own fault,' she said to herself, speaking quite audibly. 'You had a veil over your eyes which you stubbornly refused to draw aside. Alma will marry Flint now and you'll find yourself wanting to go home, just so that you won't see them together.'

It had been the same with Richard and Marlene ... No, it had not. What she had felt for Richard was infinitesimal in comparison to what she felt for Flint. And once again she was having to hide her feelings, because, owing to her own folly, she had lost Flint.

It was two days before Christmas and Kirsty had asked Liane, who was working during the morning only, and then starting her Christmas break, to do a little last-minute shopping for her in Ravensville.

'I know it'll take up some of your afternoon,' went on Kirsty, 'but there are several items I forgot——'

'It's no trouble at all,' broke in Liane, not liking her cousin's apologetic attitude. 'Have you made a list?'

The list was handed over and as soon as she had finished at the library Liane went off to do the shopping. She had the runabout, because some of the items, though light in weight, were bulky.

As soon as she reached the stationers she came face to face with Flint, who, as was usual now, greeted her with a cool,

'Good afternoon, Liane. How are you these days?'

'Fine, thanks.'

He looked at her and frowned.

'I believe the heat's rather too much for you,' he said. 'You're tired.'

Her eyes darted up to his. The concern in his voice could be the result of imagination on her part ... but she did not think so.

'I shall get used to it, as I've said.'

'You have a break now. How long?' His tone was brisk, magisterial, almost, and Liane felt a tiny thrill of pleasure run through her.

'Just over a week.'

'Why aren't you at home? This afternoon's going to be unbearably hot.'

'I'm doing a little shopping for Kirsty. It won't take long.' He seemed to look questioningly at her and she told him she had the runabout. He knew she used Kirsty's bicycle to come to work and again she wondered if his concern was real, or whether she imagined it. His next words proved that it certainly was real.

'I'm glad about that. However, if you hadn't had the runabout I'd have taken you home. A bicycle's not for this weather; you'd melt before you reached Gimbulu.' The grey eyes flickered with a hint of amusement and her pleasure multiplied a hundredfold. Flint had invited Kirsty, Mark and herself to his house on the evening of Christmas Day and she had until now been apprehensive about the visit, wondering how she would go on with Flint being so markedly cool in his attitude towards her. 'Have you much more shopping to do?' His glance was directed upwards as he spoke. 'We're in for a storm, but not for another hour or so.'

'I've finished when I've been in here,' she replied. 'Kirsty wants some paper serviettes.'

A moment later she was at the counter, having said

goodbye to Flint. The runabout was on the car park in the centre of town and within ten minutes she was pressing the starter. Nothing happened and she tried again. After about five minutes or so she was beginning to admit that there must be something wrong with the engine. She glanced around, not too happy with the heat as it had become dreadfully oppressive during the past quarter of an hour. It was most unfortunate that the runabout was out of action just at this time, as it was obvious that the storm of which Flint had spoken would not be long in coming. It was to be expected, of course, since there had been three weeks of hot, sultry weather, and no rain. The rain was desperately needed, and the farmers would be welcoming these dark cumulo-nimbus clouds which were gathering threateningly in the sky.

There was no one on the car park, and not another car. Liane glanced up again at the glowering sky and decided to return to the stationery shop and stay there until the storm came and then died down.

She was on her way there when once again she met Flint.

'The runabout's gone wrong,' she answered when he had demanded to know why she wasn't on her way home.

'Gone wrong?' he frowned. 'Where is it?' He spoke with some urgency, his eyes scanning the sky, which was becoming darker with every moment that passed.

'On the car park.'

'You've got petrol?'

'Yes, it's not anything like that.'

'I think,' decided Flint, 'that you'd better leave it there. I'd take a look at it if I thought there was time.

But I don't. My car's just along here; come, we'd better hurry.'

'The shopping's in the runabout,' she began, but Flint was already speaking, offering to collect the items which were in her vehicle. This he did, driving quickly on to the park.

'Stay where you are,' he ordered when Liane would have got out of the car with the intention of helping him to transfer the shopping from the runabout. She heard the command in his voice and felt an exciting flurry in her veins because of it.

She sat in the car, aware of the intense heat, and of clouds heavy with moisture pressing close to the earth, suffocatingly low. Her attention was caught by the dry crackling sound of the leaves as the wind began to moan in the upper branches of the trees. And even as she watched, the activity increased, the lower boughs quivering and swaying under the strengthening power of the wind. It tore through them, and the weakest began to break off and fall to the ground. From a long, long way off came the soft rumble of thunder—a faint, primitive echo, the threat of what was to come.

'We shall have to hurry.' Flint, back in the seat beside her after having put all her purchases in the boot, switched on the engine, and the lights; for over the still and silent landscape there had fallen that grim, purple-grey half-light that precedes a violent tropical storm. Scarcely had they left the car park behind when the whole sky became lit by cosmic white flashes, followed by the first sharp clap of thunder. 'There won't be time to take you to Gimbulu,' said Flint rather grimly. 'In fact, it will surprise me if we can manage to reach Kimara before the rain comes.'

By rain he meant a torrential downpour through which it would be impossible to travel. And although the first drops had not yet began to fall by the time he reached the drive to his homestead, he took no chances, but turned in, and a few moments later Liane and he were in the sitting-room, where the lights had to be put on, for the darkness was now falling rapidly as the gigantic mass of the rain-swollen storm clouds spread over the sky.

'Would you like some tea?' Flint inquired, his grey eyes examining her face. 'Sit down,' he added, indicating a chair. 'You look ready to drop.'

She had to admit that the heat was troubling her; she felt so lethargic that she could quite easily have fallen asleep. Her forehead was damp, as was her hair, and the thin white blouse she wore with a bright green cotton skirt.

'I'd love a cup of tea, thank you, Flint.' She sat down and leant back restfully. 'This is good.'

Flint rang the bell and Kamau, silent and unsmiling, entered within seconds. Flint ordered tea and cakes; Kamau brought scones as well, newly-baked and still warm. Home-made jam and fresh cream came with them and although she was not hungry Liane felt her mouth watering at such an appetising sight.

The tea was poured out by Flint, who asked her if she would like him to butter a scone for her.

'I can do it,' she laughed. 'I admit I'm tired, but I don't need waiting on.'

He shrugged and helped himself to sugar. After a space he said,

'Have you decided to settle here, in this part of Africa?'

'I haven't quite made up my mind.'

His eyes became unreadable.

'You obviously took my advice and decided not to go on cherishing hopes that would never materialise.' It was a statement, spoken with the old familiarity— and bluntness. Absurdly Liane's heartbeats quickened; it seemed ridiculous that it was his roughness and lack of thought for her feelings that lightened her spirits.

'I did decide to leave my job,' was all she offered in response to what he had said.

'And cut your losses as I told you to.' Imperious the tone, arrogant, almost. And those grey eyes were indeed like flint. 'I'm glad you've learned.'

Liane sat up and drew closer to the table.

'How long will the storm last, do you think? Kirsty will of course know that I'm not going to be out in it——' She broke off as another brilliant flash of lightning lit the heavens, then an ear-splitting clap of thunder was almost instantly followed by the first splashes of rain on the windows. Within seconds it had reached torrential proportions and for several minutes it seemed that the whole of the heavens had split in half, releasing all the water that had ever gone into them. Fascinated, Liane could only stare through the window, and gasp now and then at the savage intensity of the storm. Lightning continued to flash; thunder claps, intensified in volume, were like earth-rending explosions whose vibrations seemed to shake the very foundations of the house. Rain, flayed by the fury of the wind, lashed the roof and window-panes, and the stream which meandered through both Mark's land and that belonging to Flint, was already a foaming river.

'I never realised it could be like this,' she breathed at last in an awed tone of voice. 'You'd think that every plant would be washed away.'

'Many will be,' he told her, adding that precious topsoil would also be lost. 'However, we need the rain,' he went on, passing her the scones. 'This is Africa, Liane.' He paused a moment. 'If you do decide to live here then you'll have to get used to it.'

She accepted a scone from the plate and put it on her own.

'You're thinking that I don't like the storm?' she said, reaching for the butter.

'Do you?'

'I love it! It's all part of nature.' Her lovely eyes glowed with radiance. 'Any act performed by nature is a miracle—and I believe in miracles.' She took some butter and spread it on her scone. Flint said, passing her the jam and cream,

'You sound remarkably happy for one who has lost so much.' His tone was brusque, and tinged with sarcasm.

'I don't understand?'

'This Richard. You're not still brooding over what you've lost.'

She looked at him, attempting to read his mood. He appeared to be feigning indifference one moment, but the next he was referring to her former employer. He was slowly buttering a scone, and she found herself more than ever affected by his attractions. His firm features, bronzed and finely-chiselled, were exceptional; his bearing which spelled superiority and self-assurance—these also were exceptional. Liane caught her breath, reflecting on her folly, when she had allowed the picture of Richard to loom like a high blockade, hemming in her vision so that she could not see that her feelings for Flint were growing far beyond the bounds of mere friendship. She recalled his numerous admiring glances, his flattery ... and all she could do was wish it were Richard who was with her. Fool that she had been—holding on to the dross and allowing the gold to trickle through her fingers.

Well, she had lost Flint, and she had no one to blame but herself. Would he marry Alma? No, she was very sure he would not. The girl had tried, but Liane somehow knew she would never succeed in winning Flint for a husband.

'You haven't commented on my remark, Liane.' There was a strange unfathomable insistence in Flint's voice now and she looked bewilderedly at him across the table. Outside, the thunder continued to clap with deafening intensity, and the rain was still a deluge dropping from the grim dark sky above.

'About Richard, you mean?' He nodded his head but made no reply. And for some quite incomprehensible reason Liane felt a dart of anger, and without stopping to think she retorted, lifting her chin a little,

'I didn't lose him! He asked me to marry him, so there!'

'He——!' Flint's eyes opened very wide. 'What did you say?' he demanded almost harshly. 'Repeat it!'

His manner subdued her and for a moment she was silent.

'Richard asked me to marry him,' she said at length.

'And you refused?'

She nodded, putting down the piece of scone she

181

had in her hand. Somehow, she wasn't hungry any more.

'I found I didn't love him, after all,' she admitted, feeling rather foolish as she recalled her frank admission that she would be the happiest woman alive if she were engaged to Richard.

'I did say it was merely infatuation, if you remember?'

She nodded, swallowing uncomfortably.

'Yes, I remember,' she said.

'Do you also remember that evening, in your glade, when——?'

'Oh, please——!' She looked beseechingly at him. 'Don't remind me of that!' Distress brought a sudden brightness to her eyes. Flint noticed this and a wise little smile curved his lips.

'Why shouldn't I remind you of it?' he asked, uncaring that he might be adding to her distress. 'You've recalled it many times—— No, don't you dare deny it! I've remarked on your honesty before now——'

'Flint, what are y-you trying to say to—to me?' Her heart was racing madly, and every nerve in her body seemed to be affected by it. She had lifted her cup with the intention of taking a drink, but her hand was so unsteady that she put it down again. It met the saucer with a loud clatter which brought a hint of amusement to Flint's eyes.

'In that glade, I said it was me you loved, and not this fellow Richard.' Flint paused, his intent gaze fixed on her lovely face. 'You *have* recalled that evening many times, haven't you, Liane?' She nodded without speaking and he added, a wealth of tenderness in his voice now, 'And you've regretted the answer you gave me.' This latter was a statement, and as he made it Flint rose from the table, came round it and, taking her hand in his, he drew her gently to her feet. 'When I advised you to come over here and live, I promised not to trouble you in any way, remember?'

Liane, her heart still beating far too quickly for comfort, said yes she did remember.

'You were referring to—to your proposal ...' Liane allowed her voice to trail away to silence as Flint, not appearing to have much interest in speech for the moment, drew her to his breast, and as she lifted her face to look at him he pressed his lips to hers in a gentle tender kiss that spread warmth throughout her entire body.

'When you did return,' continued Flint when presently he held her from him, 'I remembered that promise and tried to keep it. I kept my distance although I found it most difficult, Liane.' His deep grey eyes, looking lovingly into hers, were just a little admonishing too. 'Why didn't you come to me, and tell me everything?'

'That Richard had proposed, you mean?'

'That, and also that you loved me.'

'But I thought that *you* no longer loved *me*,' she confessed, her mind leaping back to the time when she had even wondered if Flint had ever been in love with her at all. He was probably grateful that she had turned him down, she had told herself.

'Did you believe my love to have been so weak that it could have died almost immediately?' His voice was stern and censorious, and his eyes had hardened a little. 'What sort of opinion do you have of me?'

She coloured and looked down.

'I should have known better,' she admitted contritely.

'You certainly should! But then you've no sense, have you, allowing your mind to travel along that narrow single track?'

His censure was becoming a little too much for her, and she retaliated, despite the fact that she would far sooner nestle in his arms and just remain in that heavenly state for a long, long while.

'I did eventually come to my senses! I had the wisdom to turn down Richard's offer of marriage! I also made the wise and sensible decision to come out here.'

'Then you should have carried your new-found wisdom a little further, and come to me straightaway.'

'I know that now——' She smiled rather wanly up at him. 'Why didn't I remember your promise not to trouble me if ever I should come back? I'd forgotten all about it and so I believed your off-handedness was there because you didn't like me any more——'

'You idiot, Liane!' Flint gave her a little shake. 'Where love is concerned, my child, you are incredibly naïve! I might have appeared to be off-hand—and indeed I meant to be—but there were times when I just couldn't keep my eyes off you.'

She had noticed, and there had been occasions when her hopes had risen, but once in conversation with him she was subjected to that cold indifference which seemed to make her wonder if his admiring glances were nothing more than imagination on her part.

'Then there was Alma,' murmured Liane as the thought came to her.

The grey eyes were keen, discerning, as they looked into hers.

'You knew darned well that I'd never marry Alma, so

you needn't bring her in as an excuse for anything you might have neglected to do.' He paused a moment. 'I suppose I was a little attentive towards Alma. I expect I wanted to prove to you that I didn't care that you'd refused me. It was stupid of you not to guess what I was about!'

His voice was stern-edged, but his eyes were laughing.

'Aunt Miriam was troubled that you might marry her,' Liane offered as a mild defence, and again she was given a little shake.

'Aunt Miriam's a sly schemer—and you know it, my girl!'

She had to laugh, and Flint laughed with her. And he held her close to his heart for a long and rapturous interlude, kissing her now and then, sometimes with infinite gentleness, sometimes with such ardour that she was swept along with it, feeling that a tidal wave had caught her. She knew moments of exquisite rapture, moments of ecstatic fulfilment; she was in turn serene and breathless, and when at last he held her at arms' length, she heard him say, in a voice that was a strange mingling of vibrant desire and tender, gentle persuasion,

'You're going to marry me soon, my beloved?'

Liane nodded, her beautiful eyes glowing with love for him, her smile tender and very sweet.

'Just whenever you say,' she murmured softly.

'Then it will be before this year is out,' he told her, and although his tone informed her that all protestations would fall on deaf ears, she did remind him that there were only a couple of weeks to go before the new year came in.

'It's not long, really——'

'Too long,' asserted Flint imperiously. 'When this storm's abated we'll go back into Ravensville and see about a special licence. I might even manage to have you for a Christmas present!'

And as Liane was no longer inclined to offer any argument, she merely lifted her limpid blue eyes to his, and offered her lips in sweet and joyous surrender. She had come home, home to Flint, and the safe harbour of his love where she and he would dwell in simplicity and peace.

And there's still *more* love in

# Do you have a favorite Harlequin author? Then here is an opportunity you must not miss!

# HARLEQUIN OMNIBUS

Each volume contains **3** full-length compelling romances by one author. Almost **600** pages of the very best in romantic fiction for only $**2.75**

A wonderful way to collect the novels by the Harlequin writers you love best!

# What the press says about Harlequin Romances...

"...clean, wholesome fiction...always with an upbeat, happy ending."
—*San Francisco Chronicle*

"...a work of art."
— *The Globe & Mail*, Toronto

"Nothing quite like it has happened since *Gone With the Wind*..."
—*Los Angeles Times*

"...among the top ten..."
—*International Herald-Tribune*, Paris

# What readers say about Harlequin Romances

"I feel as if I am in a different world every
time I read a Harlequin."
A.T.,* Detroit, Michigan

"Harlequins have been my passport to the
world. I have been many places without
ever leaving my doorstep."
P.Z., Belvedere, Illinois

"I like Harlequin books because they tell
so much about other countries."
N.G., Rouyn, Quebec

"Your books offer a world of knowledge
about places and people."
L.J., New Orleans, Louisiana

"Your books turn my...life into something
quite exciting."
B.M., Baldwin Park, California

"Harlequins take away the world's troubles and for a while you can live in a world of your own where love reigns supreme."

L.S.,* Beltsville, Maryland

"Thank you for bringing romance back to me."

J.W., Tehachapi, California

"I find Harlequins are the only stories on the market that give me a satisfying romance with sufficient depth without being maudlin."

C.S., Bangor, Maine

"Harlequins are magic carpets...away from pain and depression...away to other people and other countries one might never know otherwise."

H.R., Akron, Ohio

*Names available on request